THE LEATHER BOYS

The Leather Boys

GILLIAN FREEMAN

A FOUR SQUARE BOOK

For Gerald Leach
(Harringay and the Old Bailey)

The Leather Boys was first published in Great Britain by Anthony Blond Ltd
in 1961, under the author's pseudonym 'Eliot George'
© Eliot George 1961

Front cover photograph by Barrie Wentzell

∎

FIRST FOUR SQUARE EDITION *The Leather Boys* by Eliot George, 1963
SECOND FOUR SQUARE EDITION *The Leather Boys* by Gillian Freeman, 1966

Four Square Books are published by The New English Library Limited. from Barnard's
Inn, Holborn, London, E.C.1. Made and printed in Great Britain by C. Nicholls & Co. Ltd.

ONE

"THEY often does a motion as they goes, dear," said the laying-out woman. She was both comic and obscene, keeping her blue felt hat on as she worked with a deftness Dick couldn't help admiring even though he felt so disgusted.

"I must give 'er credit, she kept 'im spotless," the woman said, doing things which made him turn and stare out of the window at the cluttered back yard. "Now, if you'll just give me an 'and moving 'im, we'll get 'im into 'is pyjamas."

Dick forced himself to look at the groomed and ageless corpse, and then assisted the woman in putting on the pair of striped pyjamas he remembered his mother giving to Grand-dad last Christmas. People oughtn't to do it, he thought angrily, if they can't do it by them bloody selves. He looked at the floury-faced little woman with her bony arms and almost concave chest. She was busy buttoning up the jacket. For Christ's sake get on with it, he wanted to shout at her. He's dead, isn't he?

The woman patted the arm nearest to her. "There! 'E looks very nice."

"You don't need me no more then?" Dick asked abruptly. He turned to leave the room.

"It's just a matter of settling . . ."

"I 'adn't forgotten. 'Ow much?"

"I usually ask two-pound."

Dick nodded. Money didn't matter for once. His grandparents had saved all their lives for this event, renting the double grave in the grimy little Brixton cemetery for the last forty years, keeping just enough in their dwindling post-office account to have a respectable funeral. It took precedence over everything – food, clothes, coal, even presents which they loved to give. "We don't want to be a burden to anyone when we're gone."

Why not? Use the money, have a new blanket if you want it, or a telly. Have some lino put down in that dark, dreary little

5

room you both sit in from morning to night. The argument was a waste of his emotion and energy. They weren't on the same wavelength. He would come to understand their point of view, they would say, one mustn't die ashamed. He'd be ashamed to live the way they did.

He walked out of the bedroom into the gloomy passage and opened the kitchen door. His grandmother, well over seventy and enormously fat, sat with her head in her hands, a glass of whisky on the table in front of her. There was always whisky in the medicine box.

"She wants two bloody quid," Dick said. The old woman counted out two-shilling pieces from her shabby buttoned purse.

"You'll 'ave to go down the post office and draw some more Monday."

"I'll pay, anyway," he said, "you keep your money." He wasn't short. He had worked the last few weeks, labouring on a building site, and had done overtime. Gran put her purse back into her handbag with shaking hands. It wasn't grief, Dick thought. His own hands had been shaking as he had heaved the wizened corpse. Gran's hands always shook.

The laying-out woman tapped at the door and came in.

"Well, I'm just off. I'll tell Mr. Lunnis to call."

"'Ere's your lolly," Dick said.

"Won't you 'ave a cup of tea, dear?" Gran asked. She held the belief that everyone who called must be offered refreshment or would think her uncharitable.

"Wish I could, dear, but I must get back to do me 'usband's sandwiches for 'is night shift."

Do you wash your hands first? Dick wondered. In a few moments he would have to go back into the bedroom and empty the washbasin into the slop-pail, then carry it out through the kitchen to the lavatory. Gran always insisted that the pail, an incongruous red plastic one, should be emptied down the lavatory and not the sink. When he did go back into the bedroom again, keeping his eyes away from the figure neatly tucked up in bed, he found Grand-dad's un-emptied urine bottle behind the bucket. He felt revolted and sick. His skin seemed to tighten and shrink. He wasn't sqeamish but he had never experienced such nausea as he did now, faced with death and decay. He picked up the bottle and emptied it into the slop-pail without looking at it. Then he picked up the pail and took it through the kitchen to the

6

outside lavatory where the pile of torn-up newspapers on the window-sill rustled in the draught from the door.

Gran was busy with her post-office savings book and writing things down on a piece of paper. Dick came back without the bucket.

"I was spared long enough to look after 'im," she said, crying. "It was a blessing, wasn't it, love?"

"'E couldn't have managed without you," Dick said, thinking, managed what? Dying?

Gran accepted the remark as agreement and condolence. "What should I do without you, eh? You're a good boy." It made him feel martyred and satisfied for a moment.

"'Ave you drawn the curtains in the front room?" she asked, remembering them. "We don't want no callers."

"I'll do it now." Dick went along the passage to the over-stuffed, dusty room by the front door and unlocked it. The curtains were faded cotton, so faded that the original colours of the pattern had become a uniform beige. There were rows of family photographs on the mantelpiece and pianola and a chipped china Alsatian dog on the upright piano. He drew the curtains and almost simultaneously there was a knock at the front door. He went unhurriedly to open it, thinking he hadn't drawn the curtains in time. There was a small man on the step wearing a brown trilby and a fawn belted raincoat. He took off his hat, revealing sparse sandy hair brushed in a straight line across the dome of his head from what was presumably a parting low down on the left. The hair was so greased that it appeared to consist of about ten strands, each the thickness of a blade of grass. He held the trilby at navel level and bowed over it.

"My deepest sympathy," he said soulfully. Dick stared at him. "The name is Lunnis; Frederick Lunnis, undertaker."

"Come in," Dick said. "Gran's in 'ere." He led the way into the kitchen and Mr. Lunnis introduced himself in a flurry of condolences and suddenly took a plastic wallet out of his top breast pocket, snapped it open, and like someone dealing cards placed three sepia-tinted postcard prints on the table in front of Gran.

"I do two funerals," he said, in a brisk, business patter. "For forty pounds I have this . . ." he tapped at the first photograph with a forefinger and they all looked at the picture of an upright 1930ish Austin hearse, and the four top-hatted pall-bearers

7

lifting a coffin in or out of the back. Behind it was another car, empty except for the top-hatted driver.

"For twenty pounds I do a less elaborate funeral. No mourners of course." He indicated a photograph of a small black van. "Naturally your dear soul has the full use of my Chapel of Rest." He pointed to the third photograph which showed something like a nissen hut. "Fully consecrated and in my own peaceful garden." He drew out of his wallet a colour tint of the chapel's interior and put it before them with the air of a saleswoman saying triumphantly, "I know Madam will simply *love* this."

They peered at the blurred and glossy photograph. There were highly coloured blue curtains at the end of the chapel and in front of them were some very red roses with bright green leaves. A brown coffin stood on a brown trestle table and on the coffin were more red roses tied with a ribbon. There was a dazzling white card attached to the ribbon, unless it was a flaw in the photograph.

"We want the best you got," Gran said.

Mr. Lunnis stood up. "May I see your departed before I go? I'll arrange for his removal to my Chapel of Rest later this evening. Unless you wish to keep him with you, of course." Dick said they didn't and left him in the bedroom, taking a slide rule out of his pocket.

Dick longed to be able to get away. He felt if only he could do something normal like having a drink or going to the pictures he would be able to face the night in the house, and the funeral. He kept having mental pictures of assisting with the laying out, and recollecting the confidential remarks of the woman on *rigor mortis* and running noses and not quite relevant snips of information about death.

"Funny things 'appen to people as they cross over to the other side," she had said. "A policeman friend of mine told me that when a bloke's swung, about an hour after it 'appens 'e gets an ... like a chicken running about with its neck wrung. Funny old bodies we got, ain't we?" she added affectionately.

Mr. Lunnis had returned from the bedroom. He shook hands with them both.

"Your plot is at St. Mark's, I understand. Only a short drive from my chapel. Leave all the arrangements with me. Everything will be carried out with sympathy and taste."

At the front door he said to Dick, "We'll be back with the coffin in about an hour. If you leave the door open for me the old lady needn't know what's happening. Better that way. Less upsetting."

Dick nodded. Gran would be scared stiff if she knew the front door was open. She had always been afraid of people breaking in, though what she thought anyone would break in *for* was beyond him. She had become even more nervous since she and Grand-dad had made their bedroom downstairs during his illness.

"Why don't you sleep upstairs again, Gran?" he asked her. He was sitting opposite her by the fire, in a wooden armchair with an old tartan rug draped over its hard back.

"I'd rather be in me own bed," Gran said. "I've slept in it for sixty years, and now it's downstairs, I'm down. I'm not giving it up now. Dad died in it and I will too. I'd never go into 'ospital, I've made Doctor promise. I'd rather go a bit sooner in me own 'ome, I've told 'im."

He couldn't help remarking how she said "Dad died in it", as if it hadn't been this morning. She was concerned only with herself now. Old people forgot quickly. He thought they minded about things less. Like Aunt Lily. She adored her husband but when he died she cried for a day or two, then tidied up the house, ate more heartily and drank more stout than ever before. She talked about "poor old Fred" as if he had never really lived in the place. Dick knew that in a few days Gran would refer to Grand-dad as "poor". The dead were always "poor".

"Another thing 'e's promised," Gran went on, "is to make sure I've really gone. I've always 'ad a fear being buried when I'm still 'ere."

Dick had heard all this before many times. Everything she told him now was repetitive or reminiscent. She couldn't help it but it was dead boring. He tried not to yawn. Gran talked on and he answered when he had to. He heard the door open and loud whispers in the hall, and a muffled bump as the coffin presumably turned the difficult corner into the bedroom.

"Let's put the wireless on," he said. "You don't want to miss the news."

"It ain't time for the news," Gran said. But he turned the knob and she said tearfully, "I suppose it'll take me mind off." He thought perhaps she knew what was happening after all.

"Will you stay a few days?" she asked, easing herself in the chair. "I don't fancy being on me own."

"Course I will," he said. "I'll just pop 'ome and tell Mum."

He was relieved at the idea of getting out of the house for a bit. He waited until he heard the front door close and then looked in the fly-spotted glass over the mantelpiece and combed his long hair. "Shan't be long, Gran. You 'ave a little nap."

"Ta-ta, love." She was already dozing, her head nodding down on to her chest, her chin resting in turkey-cock folds on the black bodice. Her legs were wide apart, giving her an enormous stretched lap.

He hurried along the street to the bus stop. He was quite glad he was going to have a couple of weeks at Gran's. She didn't mind what he did. She never had done. He remembered the endless sausage rolls and potato crisps and chocolates of his childhood. His own parents worried about money and the law. Gran was like him, just on the good side of it. Mum and Dad nagged him from morning to night. Gran loved him.

He lived only a mile or two away. As he got off the bus he thought how alike the streets were with the caramel-coloured varnished front doors and the dark hallways beyond, the unkempt squares of front garden, the broken gates. He pushed open his own front door.

"Mum," he called. "I'm staying up at Gran's."

His mother was still in the square-shouldered black suit she had put on that morning when the message about Grand-dad arrived. She came out into the hall and watched him without speaking, then as he went up the stairs, she said, "When's the funeral, then?"

"Tuesday."

"They taken 'im away or is 'e still in the 'ouse?"

"'E's gone to some chapel or other." Dick went into his bedroom and pulled his suitcase off the top of his wardrobe. His mother followed him into the room and watched him take his suits and shoes out of the wardrobe and his ties out of a drawer.

"Don't forget anything," she said sarcastically. "You might not 'ave enough to wear."

"I got to look smart," he said. Mum never understood clothes were important.

"Smart," said his mother. "God 'elp us." She went out.

"See you Tuesday, then," Dick called as he ran downstairs, his suitcase in his hand. But his mother had switched on the television programme his arrival had interrupted, and was too distracted to hear.

He wasn't in a hurry to get back to Gran's. He preferred it to his own home, but she fussed over him too much. Already he imagined her waiting up for him when he came in late at night – not to yell at him as his father did, but to give him a hot drink. Still, he thought, I'll have something to eat with her first, before I go out. We didn't have tea. He bought some fish-and-chips on the corner of her street, and when he got in made a strong pot of tea.

"Don't mind if I go out, do you, Gran?" he asked as they ate.

"You do what you like, love. I never been one to mind what you was up to." She added, "I never give it a thought at Christmas I'd 'ave lost 'im in six months."

"Sure you don't mind being on your own for an hour or two?"

"Got to get used to it, ain't I?" She looked at him fondly. "Per'aps you might come 'ere for good, eh?"

He went upstairs to the back bedroom to change. It was a cold room. There was a small black empty grate with a chocolate-brown surround, and a looking-glass propped up on the mantelpiece. The bed was an iron one and one of the brass knobs, the whipped-cream-walnut variety, was lost from the bedhead. The white cotton bedspread was peppered with small moth-holes and there was a lopsided washstand with a flowered basin and jug.

He poured some water into the basin and began to change. It took him a long time because he liked to look really smart. He had brought a clothes brush with him, and a shoe brush. He always took great care of his shoes, which he had hand-made and which cost him a lot of money. Tonight he was wearing a suit but sometimes he wore a narrow-shouldered jacket with plum-coloured stripes, and sometimes a leather jacket with saddle-stitching. He tied his tie carefully in front of the little looking-glass, and then bent his knees so that he could see to do his hair. It was thick and dark and wavy and grew to the tops of his ears. As he combed his hair he jutted his chin forward and narrowed his eyes. This was the mental image he carried of himself.

"Proper peacock," said Gran, half admiring, half jeering. "Out to kill tonight, ain't you. Proper toff."

TWO

"I'm going out," Reggie said.

"Do what you like. It don't worry me." His wife, Dot, turned her back. She was small and angular, her head bound up in a blue turban studded with the irregular bumps of her curlers. She inhaled a thin cigarette and Reggie thought how she smelt of smoke and how her clothes and his clothes and their room smelt of smoke. When he kissed her, which wasn't often, it was as if her open mouth suddenly exhaled a store of stale smoke and it tasted acrid and unpleasant. He wished he had never married her. They were both eighteen.

He pulled on his big leather motor-cycling jacket and went out to his bike, which was propped against the kerb. He climbed on and kicked the starter, all his frustration and boredom and disappointment venting itself. It was a warm night. The fluorescent lamplights made the pavements orange and the faces of passers-by green and grey. Not many people were out except boys and girls of his own age. Cats, he called them to himself. I wonder how many of the cats are around tonight? They met at a café called Nick's. It was a workmen's café in the daytime, quite ordinary, but at night it was different. It acquired, for them at least, an excitement and a glamour. It was the café for the boys on motor-bikes. It was like a badge of admittance, the bike and the gear. It gave Reggie his only sense of belonging and being part of society. The gear was made of leather: leather trousers, leather jackets, leather gloves. It was extremely expensive, usually made individually to the wearer's own design and ideas. It was fashionable and yet it seemed to the boys who wore it more than a fashion. It made them feel important. They felt select. They were proud. All their money went on the bike or the clothes. The girls liked to see them in leather, they liked to wear it, to have this feeling of separateness and power. Other people were frightened or attracted. Some men came along dressed in the whole kit,

12

yet Reggie knew they hadn't motor-cycles, but cars parked a mile down the road. The boys laughed at them. They called them "kinky", and "the leather johnnies", but some of them went off with them. They said it was good for an easy quid or two. Reggie had never tried it himself.

As he turned the corner into the main street he could hear the noise; giggling, shouting, bikes revving. One of the boys was circling his bike in the road, round and round and round. Reggie tore to a standstill and parked his bike and pushed through the group in the doorway. He went over to the counter and bought a bottle of Cola and sat down at the nearest table. Two of the girls came and sat down with him.

"You coming with us tonight, Reggie?" one asked him.

"I might." He didn't want to go home. "Where you going?"

"Up the club. There's dancing."

It was good for a laugh if nothing else, all that orangeade and buns and the Vicar trying to look as if he was happy.

"I might," he said again. He looked towards the door and saw Dick come in and thought, I've seen him before. At first he couldn't remember where, and then he remembered that it was in a cinema queue about a month before. He had been with Dot, and this bloke had been with a fat old girl with ankles like beer cans. They had even spoken, something about the bloody long queue for tickets. At first he had thought Dick was one of their lot, because of his jacket. Dick saw him, hesitated, then came over.

"Hi."

"Hi," said Reggie. He stood up and went over to the counter with Dick.

Dick said. "Who the chicks?" He didn't care but it was the expected line of conversation.

"Oh, they just 'ang around the joint. D'you fancy 'em?"

Dick turned and stared at the two girls sitting at the table Reggie had just left. Their skirts – one was black leather – ended above their thin black-stockinged knees.

"No, mate." They didn't attract him. Long strings of beads hung down between their separated breasts. Their lipstick was very pale and shiny.

"You 'aven't been down 'ere before," Reggie said.

"I don't live 'ere," Dick explained. "I'm staying with me Gran. I just come out to 'ave a look round and see where to go."

Reggie nodded.

13

"What you doing tonight then, after?"

"Not much to do, is there?" said Dick.

"You could come with us, mate."

"Where to?"

"Up the youth club."

"I don't go for them," Dick said. "We got one where I live, table tennis and all that."

"Ping-pong," drawled Reggie affectedly. They both laughed, and sat down at the nearest empty table. The girls followed them, giggling and talking provocatively, watching the boys to see their reaction. Reggie said, "I wish you birds'd shut it. We can't 'ear ourselves think." They moved off haughtily and Reggie turned to Dick. "You got a bike, then?"

Dick shook his head. Until now he hadn't really wanted one of his own. There was always his father's.

"I 'ave. I got it outside."

They shoved and elbowed their way to the street again where the motor-cycle stood in the middle of the row. To Dick Reggie's looked the same as all the others.

"'Ow fast can it go?"

"A ton easy." Dick was impressed. He thought perhaps he might go in for one himself. If he worked regularly he could pay for it without trouble. He earned up to eighteen pounds a week with overtime. The thing was he didn't like to work all the year round. It was the thought of paying the weekly amount which depressed him. Mum and Dad paid off all the time. Each week, when Dad brought home his wage packet, Mum peeled off the notes that were mortgaged for the television, the put-u-up, Dad's own motor-cycle combination. Dick liked to feel the money fat in his pocket. Then he could go and buy a suit or shoes or go drinking. Better than Dad's pint on a Sunday. It was living. Besides, things like having his hair done cost money – ten bob a time at least, more if he had it styled. He liked to have it styled quite often. There were more men's hairdressers than women's now, in the district where he lived, the windows filled with photographs of men with elaborate hair styles. For poufs, his mother said. But it wasn't true. All the kids went. Just because, when Dad was his age, no one had the money to spend on themselves, his parents thought it was wrong. Dad was never smart, his clothes were terrible, flapping grey trousers that would fit an elephant. Mum's clothes were awful too. He glanced back at the lighted café. Even those dim birds knew how to dress.

14

"Want a ride?" Reggie asked.

"Don't mind." Dick really wanted to. "Does it cost a lot to run it?"

"About three quid a week. Depends 'ow much extra you want for it."

"You got a lot extra?"

Reggie nodded. "These lights. This aerial. It doesn't do anything, but it looks good, like a speed cop's. And plenty of gear for meself." He pulled on his big leather gloves and climbed on to the saddle. Dick put his leg over the pillion. Several boys who had been larking about in the road ran on to the pavement and stood in a group laughing noisily and shouting insults and advice.

"Don't forget red means stop, mate."

"Count the bodies, mate."

Dick, with a sudden shock, like a pin puncturing the balloon of his enjoyment, remembered his grandfather. He shouted to Reggie, who was revving the engine, "My grand-dad bought it this morning."

"Wish mine 'ad," Reggie answered. "Crafty old bugger."

They swung into the middle of the road.

"Where to, mate?"

"Let's try that club, then."

The night air cut past them like the V of foam at the stern of a ship. Reggie's black jacket billowed out, porpoise-like. Dick's hair blew behind his ears as forcefully as when the hairdresser shampooed it over the back headrest of the basin.

"Smashing," Dick said, as, exhilarated, he dismounted.

The street seemed still and silent after the noise of the engine, then they became aware of the sound of voices and music from the church hall which lay back from the pavement down a short gravel drive.

"Let's go," Reggie said. He wheeled the bike down the drive and propped it against the wall of the building. They walked up two shallow steps to the gothic door. An amateur poster was pinned on it. *Dance*, it said. *Bring your records. Not square. All cats welcome on these tiles!* Underneath was a poor drawing of a couple in jeans, jiving.

"Christ!" Reggie said.

"This is a church, mate."

"Where else better, mate?"

They laughed and Dick pushed the door open and they went in. On the threshold they stopped and surveyed the room. About ten couples were doing half-hearted contortions to the swing record which was being played on an old-fashioned walnut-wood radiogram. An unmade-up woman in a royal-blue woollen dress was standing beside it, another record in her hand. Six lights hung down from the rafters on long flexes, the bulbs unshaded except for glass shields shaped like cornets. Posters, similar to the one outside, decorated the brick walls. The Vicar was dancing with a teenage girl in a black skirt, black sweater and black stockings.

"Sexy, ain't it," said Dick.

"Needs livening up," said Reggie. "Let's get the boys."

They turned abruptly and slammed the door behind them.

"They'll be expecting us," Reggie said.

"Do you think they'll get the law in?"

"What for? We ain't done nothing."

"Yet."

"Did you see their faces? That bird with the record come all over nerves. She was shaking."

It was with tremendous excitement that they raced back to the crowded café.

"Come on, cats," Reggie yelled, not turning off the engine of his bike, but keeping one foot on the road. "There's a dance at the club. It's dead, man."

Cheering, shouting, they mounted their bikes in ones and twos. Several climbed into the back of an old car with drawings and objects all over it. With high-pitched whoops they drove off fast all together.

The dance was ending as they burst into the hall. They stood silently, staring, not moving, yet somehow on the point of moving like preying animals, fifteen or twenty boys wearing motor-cycle kit. Their hair was greased and combed into styles called *College Cut* and *Latin Cut* and *Campus Cut* and *Perry Como*. Their expressions were contemptuous and excited. A record of "Good Night, Sweetheart", sung by Vera Lynn, was being amplified by the loudspeaker equipment attached to the wall above the door.

Someone shouted derisively, "Call that dancing?"

"My mum could do better."

"Come on, Dad, move your fat arse."

One of them, the boy who owned the car, suddenly seemed to become the leader. He was nearly six foot, heavily built, with a fleshy white face. His jacket had a tiger's head painted on the

16

back, his black leather jeans were stuffed into ex-army dispatch-rider's boots. He moved swiftly to the radiogram and, swinging his leg back, brought his boot crashing into the fan-shaped grill, splintering the wood and tearing the beige canvas material behind it.

The other boys surged forward on to the floor. Six of them paired and started to jive. Another used the panelling of the door as a sounding board to beat out a rhythm.

"Come on," yelled the leader, Les. "Let's do it over."

He picked up a folding wooden chair and brought it down on top of the gramophone. The Vicar advanced with his palms outstretched as if to calm them down.

"Boys, boys. Please. Let's not have any of this rough stuff."

"Want to dance, then?" Les shouted. He seized the outstretched hands and forced the Vicar into a grotesque parody of rock-an'-roll.

Dick and Reggie ran from one side of the hall to the other, seizing the chairs and swinging them against the wall. Then, breathless, they ran side by side into the little room which was used as a kitchen and began to hurl the crockery on to the floor.

The Vicar followed them, protesting. Somebody grabbed him by the collar of his jacket and pulled him round.

"'Ere, Vicar, 'ave a drink," he shouted, and emptied a milk bottle over his head. The milk cascaded down his forehead and over the lense of his glasses, and for a moment his eyes were obscured by two opaque white screens.

"Please, please, boys," he pleaded ineffectually. He was scarcely heard through the jeering and the din of smashing cups.

Louder and more effective came the shout of "Law!" from the hall. Immediately they abandoned their destruction. Some made a dive for the door. Two climbed up and lifted the sash of the window and scrambled out into the darkness. Reggie grabbed Dick's arm. "Come on, on the bike."

They ran down the length of the hall, past the shattered gramophone and debris of broken chairs and out into the small forecourt to the bike. Figures were running in all directions, up and down the road to their parked machines, briefly illuminated by the occasional street lamps. Engines were started up and motor-cycles were moving off rapidly without lights. Les's car, filled with boys, had already disappeared. Dick and Reggie tore away as a solitary policeman arrived on a light motor-cycle.

Dick put his arms round Reggie's waist and held him tightly as they accelerated fiercely away.

"What a carve-up," Reggie shouted, turning his head so that Dick could hear him. "They won't 'ave another dance there for some time."

The wind cut into their faces, obliterating their words, making their eyes water.

"Dead right they won't."

Reggie turned into the main shopping street and slowed down for the first time.

"I'll get off 'ere," Dick said.

Reggie stopped outside a big general store. The windows were brightly lit and dress dummies, draped with small pieces of sheeting, stared out with vacant modesty.

"Scared we might smash the glass and rape 'em."

Reggie laughed.

"Well, I'll be seeing you, mate," Dick said.

"Right, mate." Their eyes met. They were both suddenly ashamed. Dick wanted to say something, but didn't know how to express his feelings. He was contrite, but incoherent. He had never taken part in a similar raid, and now the excitement was over he wondered how he could have been so mean, spoiling a harmless dance organized by a well-meaning vicar. At the time he hadn't felt sorry at all. It was funny how violent he had felt, how urgent his desire to destroy.

Reggie had broken up innocent activities before. He'd been with the gang on another occasion when they had surprised a young necking couple, and terrified them, standing there with open flick knives, humiliating the man by jeering obscenities at his girl-friend, whom he was powerless to defend. He had also fought in a cinema. Each time he had loathed himself for joining in. Why did he do it? Christ, he didn't know. He had to do something, evening after evening, compelled to go out because he couldn't stay home with Dot or sit in their rented room, arguing and miserable.

"Well, cheerio, then." Dick turned and walked hurriedly away. He heard Reggie turn the bike and drive in the other direction. He thought irrelevantly, that it was worse because Grand-dad had died this morning. Somewhere in his mind the Vicar and Grand-dad's soul were linked. And yet, he thought, Grand-dad wasn't so lily-white either. He'd been inside twice for housebreak-

18

ing and had once assaulted a policeman when he was drunk. Not like Dad. Dad was so bloody straight it made you sick. Dad wouldn't nick a loaf if he was starving. Dad wouldn't fight if a copper was kicking him up the arse.

He opened the gate of his grandmother's house and knocked on the glass panel of the door. Gran had pasted brown paper behind the glass. He heard the kitchen door open, and then the sound of Gran's bulk shuffling down the passage, her clothes brushing the wallpaper on either side, her feet heavy but uneven on the lino. She rattled the chain out of its keep, calling out, asking if it was him. He shouted that it was and she opened the door. She was ready for bed, her hair brushed down on to the shoulders of her stained red dressing-gown, her teeth out. Her chin had lost at least an inch. Her lips met like a nutcracker.

"'Ave a good time?" she asked.

"It was all right." Dick couldn't look at her.

"Where did you go then?"

"Down Nick's caff. I met up with some blokes."

"I bet there was some girls too." She nudged him with her whole arm. "Come and 'ave a cup of tea, sweet'eart. I just made some."

The house in which Reggie and Dot lived was in darkness. He coasted silently down the road so that the landlady couldn't complain in the morning that she had to take a sleeping pill because he had woken her out of her first sleep. He opened the gate with one hand, holding the bike with the other, then bounced the bike up the kerb and wheeled it into a little shed in the garden.

He took his key out of his pocket and fitted it into the front-door lock, turning it slowly and holding it while he pushed open the door, then taking it out, holding the lock with his thumb, so that there would be no click. Very quietly he closed the door, and tiptoed along the passage and up the stairs, waiting on each step. The house smelt stuffy and slightly mouldy, a kind of sour, old bread smell mixed with dust. There was dust everywhere, along the skirting, on the picture rails, on the tops of doors. When the doors were closed you could see a growth of black fluff between the tops and the frames.

His room, his and Dot's, faced the top of the stairs. It was the best room in the house and when he had taken it, the week before they had married, he had felt it was the next best thing to a flat of their own. He hadn't felt he was letting Dot down. The double bed was against one wall and the light over it was operated by a cord which dangled from a breast-like protuberance below the picture rail. The wardrobe, made of varnished box-wood, was at the foot of the bed, and along the opposite wall was a table with a formica top and two elaborate modern kitchen chairs – these were their own property, their only furniture – a chest of drawers and a small enamel sink. Their washing things, as well as two saucepans and a frying pan, stood on the wooden draining board. In the centre of the room, facing at angles, were two armchairs covered in light brown rexine. One had a stained antimacassar on the back, the other two cigarette burns on an arm.

Dot was asleep in bed. In the lamplight which came through the window she looked almost attractive. Her hair was out of curlers and her pale skin appeared translucent and delicate, the spots on her forehead and chin invisible. Reggie undressed without much noise. Before he cleaned his teeth he opened the chest of drawers and felt under Dot's collection of petticoats for the round, pink, unlabelled tin which usually contained the contraceptive from the Family Planning Clinic. It was empty. That meant Dot was wearing it – it had to be worn for eight hours after intercourse – and she must have had a boy-friend in when he was out. He didn't care about that. He wanted to know so that if Dot woke him in the night he could rightfully refuse to make love to her. He'd do it if she was desperate, but otherwise he preferred not to. She woke him most nights, if not to perform, to get him to hand her the tin of sweets on the bedside table. She sucked toffees and crunched boiled sweets for hours. She never cleaned her teeth, and Reggie, who had been brought up by very poor, but very respectable, clean-living parents, was disgusted by her. He couldn't imagine why he had ever wanted to kiss her or lie close to her. He had married her a year ago. His mother was dead, and he and his father lived together in two rooms quite close to the one they had now. Dot's parents had wanted them to marry and had given them the expensive kitchen table and chairs as a wedding present. Dot wanted them to marry. Reggie almost wanted them to marry. He felt his life wasn't fulfilled as it was. He accepted marriage as the alternative to what he had already. It certainly wasn't physical desire. Like all his friends he had had intercourse since he was sixteen. But he knew he had to marry some time. Everyone did. So why not now? More than half of his friends were married, some of them because they had to. His father didn't mind either way.

"Do what you like, Reggie. I don't mind. Do what makes you 'appier."

He knew now that it didn't. Sometimes he thought he would get divorced, but he wasn't sure how to go about it. Still, when he really wanted to he would find out.

Dot stirred in bed and murmured, "That you, Reggie?"

"Yeah." He scrubbed at his teeth and spat into the flat scarred sink, rinsed his mouth with a teacup, and climbed into bed.

THREE

"'Ow long are you staying up 'ere?" Dick's mother asked him in a sharp whisper, her expression combining jealousy and a desire to save.

"As long as Gran wants me," he said piously. "She's on 'er own."

"We all know that, stupid. We just 'ad to fork out on the wreath."

They both turned their heads towards the car window and tried to see it, resting, with one from Gran and a few other small floral tributes, on the roof of the hearse. They were riding with Gran and Dick's father in Mr. Lunnis's first car, and the rest of the family were packed into the one behind. There was Grand-dad's tippling octogenarian brother, Dick's two uncles, an aunt and one cousin. The cousin, Rose, was a thin, sallow, sexy girl of sixteen whose black mourning dress was far from seemly.

The cars crawled to a stop outside the red-brick Victorian gothic church, and the four pall-bearers in their greasy top hats solemnly heaved the coffin to their shoulders and carried it into the church. There was no lighting inside, only the diffused light which came through the sentimental stained-glass windows in segments of ruby red, royal blue and urine yellow.

The family shuffled to the two front pews and arranged themselves. The Vicar, who had married Dick's parents and hadn't seen them since, spoke a few words of sympathy, then, mounting the steps to the altar, read a short prayer. When his voice finally echoed away they sang a hymn, their voices sounding feeble in the big empty church. Dick's Uncle Arthur sang in a strident, tuneless baritone, but everyone else breathed and mumbled the words. It was with relief that they followed the Vicar and the coffin into the cemetery, down a path between rows of gravestones, some new and gravelly white, as if castor sugar had been frosted into the stone, others black and smooth with age, the inscriptions completely gone. Little jars of daffodils stood on one or two plots. On others yesterday's wreaths were withering. A pot of plastic lilies decorated one without a headstone.

They grouped at the open grave. The coffin was suspended on broad bands of tape and lowered down as they prayed, down between the wet stony banks of earth, landing with a slight bump Dick's father shovelled on some earth, then the two uncles followed him in turn. Dick was anxious in case he should be offered the trowel too. He didn't want to. The earth was damp and he had on his best suit. But the funeral was over, and talking in muted voices, that were to break into hilarity as soon as they were out of the churchyard, they walked back to the cars.

In the car Arthur made a joke. The women and the men had separated for the ride back to Gran's, and the men felt free to laugh. Dick laughed with them, although he never really enjoyed this sort of coarse humour. Arthur's joke had been about Rose's tight black dress. "I though 'er tits was going to pop out when she knelt down."

"You wasn't sitting be'ind 'er like I was," said Dick's father.

Rose's father said defensively, "All the girls dress like that nowadays." Dick hadn't even noticed the dress was tight.

The car stopped outside Gran's front gate, and the car with the women in it drew up immediately afterwards. They climbed out and waited for Gran to unlock the front door. She found her key in her handbag, turned it in the lock, pushed the door open and waddled down the hall, the family following her in single file. At the kitchen door she turned and said, "Not in 'ere, in the front room," and they all turned back again.

Dick helped Gran off with her coat and took it into the bedroom. He opened her wardrobe and took out a hanger and hung the coat on it. It was her best coat and he thought it ought not to lie about, getting crumpled and dusty. It was a silk coat, with velvet facing on the collar. Gran had had it a long time. When she had charred she had acquired several rather grand items of clothing from her employers. Dating even further back were a silk umbrella with an ivory handle and three small petit-point evening bags. In those days Grand-dad had been a chauffeur, driving an early Benz, wearing a peaked hat, a navy tunic with silver buttons, breeches and polished black gaiters.

It was after this period – their one rather splendid period with its reflected grandeur – after the First World War, that Grand-dad had, as Gran put it, "gone down". He lost an eye in the war, damaged an ear-drum and couldn't find a regular job.

Dick closed the wardrobe door and went into the kitchen where Gran was putting food on a tray. She had bought plentifully for today. She enjoyed a party. Dick had drawn the money for her and carried the bags home. There were little pork pies and pickles, ham rolls, sausage rolls, Devonshire splits oozing imitation cream and thin jam, and a dozen cream horns, small cornucopias of leaden pastry filled with custard cream. Arthur had gone out to the off-licence earlier and fetched the beer – it was now nearly four o'clock – and when Dick carried the plates into the front room they were all drinking and jolly and ready for a good feed.

"And just 'ow long do you mean to stay off work," Dick's mother asked him, as if they were carrying on the morning's conversation.

"I might get a job soon," he said.

"You registering at the labour exchange?"

"'Course," he said, "or I wouldn't get unemployment benefit, would I?"

"Don't tell me there's no work going," his mother said, disbelievingly.

"I 'aven't took what they've offered me," Dick said.

Rose had been standing beside them, listening, nibbling a ham roll and leaving lipstick marks on the bread.

"Don't you 'ave to?" she asked.

"No, not for a couple of times. I say it's too far from me 'ome, or something like that."

"It's different for me," she said, "being an usherette. I don't 'ave to take nothing else. Either they get me a job usheretting or I don't 'ave one at all."

"Where are you working?" Dick's mother asked. "Or 'aven't you got a job now?"

"Oh yes, I'm at the Rex, A.B.C. circuit."

"Ever get any riots," Dick asked; "breaking up the place, you know?"

"Oh no," said Rose, "we don't 'ave any of those sort of pictures. Anyway, it's a nice district."

"What you got on now?" He felt it was his duty to keep the conversation going.

"Can't remember," said Rose thoughtfully. "It's lovely, though."

24

Dick pursued. "What you got coming next week?"

Dick's mother misinterpreted his persistence. "You ought to go to Rose's cinema, Dick."

"I'll put you in the three-and-sixes," Rose said. "I might even sit beside you if you're good."

"No good 'is being good, is it?" said Arthur, joining them. "Now 'oo's ready for another glass of beer?"

Gran went to sleep and the rest of them played Newmarket and Pontoon. The front room became full of smoke and Dick went into the kitchen and washed up the plates and glasses. Rose followed him and dried up with a damp tea towel.

"'Asn't she got another cloth?" she asked. "The things get all smeary with this old rag." She held out the faded towel, thin from countless dryings and years of wear.

"She don't 'ave money for those sort of things," Dick said. "She's on the pension, remember?"

"Terrible, isn't it," Rose said; "what they 'ave to live on, I mean, when you think what we spend."

"Shocking," Dick agreed.

"I expect she'll go into one of those old people's 'omes now."

"Gran? No, not 'er. Not likely."

"Well, why ever not? She'll only be a burden to the family if she sticks 'ere. Suppose she gets ill or something?"

"Wait till it 'appens," said Dick shortly.

"Some of those 'omes are very nice. Dad wants 'er to go in one."

"Some of them aren't," Dick said. "*This* is 'er 'ome. She likes it 'ere."

"Well, I can't think why," said Rose tartly. "It's a stinking 'ole, everything falling to bits."

"That's better than everything so bleeding new you can't move," Dick answered. It was like that at home. Mustn't leave fingermarks on the paint, mustn't sit on the chairs, mustn't touch the telly. Things were bought at such personal sacrifice that they gave little pleasure, only worry. He preferred it at Gran's. He preferred the Victorian crumbling to the contemporary gloss.

"Anyway," said Rose, as they went back to the front room, where the party was riotous, all thoughts of its cause forgotten, "she can't go on living 'ere on 'er own for good, can she?"

25

"I might live 'ere myself," said Dick flatly.

"You'll go crazy," Rose said, surprised. "Whatever do you want to live 'ere for?"

"I like it," said Dick. He thought of Nick's and Reggie and the boys. "I've got friends."

"A girl-friend you mean, I bet!"

"No, I don't."

"You got a girl, Dick?"

"No."

"I bet!"

Dick shrugged. She could disbelieve him if she wanted to, and she obviously wanted. He'd never had a girl-friend. Sometimes his mother half sneered at him as he was dressing to go out. "Think the girls will be after you, I suppose." But one didn't only dress up for girls. One didn't only have clean shoes and a brushed suit because one wanted girls to admire one. His appearance mattered to himself. The time he spent on it was entirely for his own satisfaction. Well, perhaps not entirely. Some was for the other boys, in peacock competition. They were the ones who judged and criticized and appraised.

In the front room Dick's mother was waiting for them.

"Why don't you go out?" she asked. "You don't want to stick round 'ere, moping."

"'Oo's moping?" Dick said. "All that's missing is the paper 'ats."

"That's right," Arthur said, ignoring Dick. Perhaps he hadn't heard. "You're only young once, as they say."

"We might as well," Rose urged. "Come on, Dick, show us the bright lights."

Dick didn't care either way. Whatever he did, it wasn't like being on his own. "I'll take you up a caff I know," he said. "There's a juke."

"Let's go, man," said Rose archly.

Reggie was sitting there with his back to the door. Dick had recognized his crew cut, and the brass studs on the epaulettes of his jacket. In any case he had seen the bike outside. He knew the difference now between Reggie's machine and the others. For some reason he felt ashamed of Rose. He didn't know why, because she was as smart as any of the girls in the café. Her tight dress, black stockings and big ear-rings were the accepted uniform. Perhaps she was a bit too posh, a bit too pleased with herself.

26

"Not a bad dump," she said grudgingly, as they sat down at a table. She tilted her chair back on two legs and surveyed the room. "'Oo do you know?"

Dick looked round. Les was at the counter with two boys who had taken part in the raid the other night.

"Them," he said, pointing. He indicated Reggie's back. He was alone. "'Im."

"Well, let's join 'im," Rose said. "We don't want to sit on our own, do we?"

Unwillingly Dick picked up his glass and led the way to Reggie's table. Reggie looked up, obviously pleased.

"'Allo, mate," he said. "I didn't see you come in."

"This is Rose," said Dick.

"Hi," smirked Rose.

"'Allo," said Reggie. She reminded him of Dot and he disliked her at once. Dick wouldn't do himself any good, hanging around with a tart like her.

"All on your own?" Rose said to him.

Reggie nodded without interest.

"'E's a lone wolf," Dick said.

"You're dead right there, mate."

Dick put his elbows on the grey mottled plastic table-top, holding his unbreakable glass in both hands.

"What's up tonight?"

"Don't know. F...... all. Les is 'ere, though."

"I know. I saw 'im." They turned to look at Les, not in his motor-cycling kit, which he wore although he drove a car, but in a suit with a metal thread running through the material, and big, grey suède shoes. As they watched him he called his girl over to him with a jerk of his head. She had dyed white-blonde hair and thick black pencil lines round her eyes. Her lashes were stuck together into spikes. She came towards him, walking in what she obviously thought to be a provocative manner. Almost without speaking, by the movements of his head and an odd monosyllable, he conveyed to her that he wanted her to go with him. She followed him out of the café, both unconsciously acting out to themselves and to each other the mannerisms they had seen in countless films. As they disappeared into the street there was a tumult of catcalls and whistles.

"Will 'e come back later?" Dick asked.

"'E might."

"Come on," Dick said to Rose. "Let's go." He was bored with

27

her and regretted having brought her here.

"I'll come back later," he said to Reggie. Rose finished her drink.

"You're in an 'urry, aren't you?" But her tone was not reproachful.

They went out and she put her arm through his. "What was you in such an 'urry for?" she asked.

Dick stiffened. He found her totally unattractive. She pressed close to him, walking so that their thighs touched. Her warmth seemed to creep through his clothes. He tried to walk faster, but her weight on his arm slowed their pace. She walked lingeringly. "No 'urry now, is there?" she said.

"No." He shook his head.

He was unaroused by her nearness, even repelled by it. She took her arm out of his and put it round his waist, slipping her hand into his trouser pocket. He let his arm hang limp but it was uncomfortable and squashed to his side. Partly because he didn't want to offend her, he put it round her. She let her head rest on his shoulder.

"I'm glad I 'ad to come today," she whispered. "I didn't want to. I thought I'd be ever so upset. But I'm glad now."

"Are you?" he said.

"Otherwise I mightn't 'ave seen you again. You was only a kid last time."

"I don't remember," he said.

She stopped walking suddenly and turned towards him passionately. "Kiss me, Dickie."

Horrified, his mouth touched hers, and her lips seemed to grow like the fleshy tentacles of a sea anemone and draw him into the wet, dark, devouring cavity within. He tried to draw away, but she clung to him, her body flattened to his, her arms and her legs and her mouth holding him.

At last she relaxed, panting, and let her head loll on his chest. "That was lovely," she said.

He was shaken and disgusted. "Come on, Rose, they'll wonder where we are." He took her hand, and almost running led her along the streets to Gran's house. At the door she took out her scented handkerchief and wiped his mouth.

"There," she whispered tenderly. "We don't want them to know, do we?"

He stood with Gran at the door, calling good-bye. Rose and

her mother waved through the amber plastic window of the motor-cycle combination side-car, slung low over the gutter. Arthur was striding down the street, shouting to Rose's father, who was putting on his goggles before climbing on to the saddle. He was a small man and his goggles turned him into a bullfrog.

"Keep cheery, Mum," Arthur shouted. "We'll all be round to see you."

Dick's parents were the last to leave. "Only wish we 'ad room for you at 'ome, Mum."

"I'm all right," Gran said, "I'm 'appier on me own."

"Well, Dick's with you for a while," Dick's father said, as if it had been his doing. "'E'll see you're all right. 'E'll tell us if you want anything."

"That's right," Dick's mother agreed.

They kissed her briefly and dryly on her cheek and walked away with brisk steps, self-satisfied and neat.

"Poor old Gran," Dick said. "I'll make a pot of tea, shall I?"

"Trying to put me in an 'ome," Gran grumbled. "That's what they've been on at me about all day."

"I won't let them," Dick promised. "You'll leave this 'ouse over my dead body."

"Rose make a set at you?" Gran asked, her mind going from one thing to another, as it always did. "Could see 'er eyeing you."

Dick said, "No." He didn't want to remember it.

"Can't fool me," Gran said. "I saw your face when you come in just now. I know that look. And Marie's." She was getting muddled. Marie was Rose's mother.

"You mean Rose," Dick said.

"Didn't I say Rose?" Gran asked. "Me memory's not good any more. I'm getting old." She looked ground greedily. "Let's 'ave some of those rolls with our tea, love. There's a plate left over."

FOUR

The café was much quieter. It was half past twelve, nearly closing time. Most of the girls had gone, and some of the boys too. Les was there, his arm round Carol, the girl with the dyed hair. Reggie was still there, not by himself now, but with four or five other boys, standing in a restless predatory group. Dick pushed open the door. The neon lighting was very bright and made him blink. Outside it was a starless and moonless night. He walked over to Reggie.

"Hi," he said

Reggie stared at him. "What you come back for?"

"What do you mean, what for?"

"Thought you was fixed for tonight. What you done with the bird?" His voice was hostile.

"She's gone 'ome."

"Quick, weren't you?"

"What do you mean, quick? She's my cousin, mate."

"That don't make no difference. Les 'as 'ad 'is sister," boasted a boy with hair shaved close to his head.

"I'm not Les," Dick said sharply. "Blimey, can't I take a bird out without telling you first?"

"Les 'ad Carol in the back of 'is car," said the shaved boy enviously.

"Well, I didn't 'ave Rose nowhere," retorted Dick. "She ain't my type."

Reggie thawed a little. "Coming with us, mate?"

"Where to?"

"Les 'asn't told us yet."

"Okay," said Dick. "I'm not doing nothing." He began to feel excited. What was Les planning for tonight? In his metallic suit and narrow, hand-painted tie he was the absolute leader, deliberately witholding from them what they were anxious to

30

know. He stood there, half embracing Carol, then, suddenly, he took her arm and twisted it.

"Ow, you sod!" she shouted. "What d'you do that for?"

He didn't answer and walked away from her to Dick and Reggie and the other boys.

"I've got something *real* on tomorrow."

"Nothing tonight, then?" asked Shaved Head disappointedly.

"I'm busy tonight," Les said. They whistled. "It's tomorrow I got plans for." He paused dramatically. "You know old Siddons down Verney Road?" He was referring to the janitor of the school most of them had attended. "You know it was 'im 'oo shopped me when I broke them windows? What got me on probation?" They murmured that they did. "It's about time 'e knew what I think of 'im, then," Les threatened. "'E's gone away for a week, my brother said. I thought we'd smash 'is place up a bit. Give 'im something to come 'ome to, like." Without waiting for them to answer he swaggered to the door. "See you all 'ere tomorrow."

They watched him climb into his car, with its rusted mudguards and yellow doors and false red chimney-pot.

"Christ," said Reggie. "We 'ang around all night and then 'e tell us to run off 'ome."

The lights were switched off, then on again.

"Good night, kids," said the café owner, coming from his back room behind the counter. "Bedtime."

"Drop me 'ome?" Dick said to Reggie.

"I'm not going 'ome."

"Where you going then?"

"Coming?"

"Okay, man." Dick didn't want to go home either.

They went silently out to the street and slowly Reggie put on his crash helmet and gloves and climbed on to his bike. Dick sat on the pillion.

"Where you going?" he asked again.

"Dunno." He kicked the starter. "Ever been to Primrose 'Ill?"

"No." Dick shouted, as the engine began to reciprocate noisily.

"We'll go there, then."

As they raced through the deserted streets he wondered why he had said it. Primrose Hill was where Dot's parents lived, behind the hill, close to Chalk Farm, in a shabby square full of children and prams and dustbins. The area in the middle, meant for flowers and grass, had been concreted over and the dust rose and the children ran and it was never quiet. Some of the surrounding streets were becoming quite posh – mauve front doors and council improvement grants for bathrooms and windows and opening up damp and unsafe basements – but Dot's square was as depressing and peeling and crumbling as it had been for the last thirty years.

He and Dot had done their courting on Primrose Hill. On hot summer Sunday afternoons they had necked for hours on the much-trodden grass.

Dick said, "Where's that then?"

And he answered, "Down Camden Town way," and accelerated. He was fed up, more fed up than he remembered feeling in his life. Everything bored him, his job in a garage, Dot, the gang. He went regularly to Nick's because he couldn't stay indoors, but he thought he hated Les, and he didn't enjoy the bullying and the raids in which he took part. In retrospect he didn't enjoy them at all. The thought of organized breaking-in and breaking-up disgusted him, although he knew he would be doing it again tomorrow night. If he didn't he wouldn't be able to go to Nick's, and if he didn't go there, where could he go?

He slowed down and drove into Regent's Park, obeying the twenty-miles-an-hour limit. Everything was dark, only illuminated briefly by his headlights. The Adam terraces were unlit. On the roofs the small standing stone figures showed even darker against the dark sky. He cruised gently for a while and then turned across the little bridge and out into Prince Albert Road, where one or two cars drove by very fast, and lights shone in windows of the big blocks of flats. At the foot of Primrose Hill he stopped.

"We've come a bloody long ride," said Dick. But he didn't mind. He loved to be on the pillion, carried through the night. While he was riding he forgot about everything, only enjoyed the sensations of speed and wind and noise. Reggie got off the bike. They were aware of the silence and stood for a moment or two.

"Come on, mate," Reggie said. "This way, mate." And Dick followed him up the steep path.

"You can see miles in the day, all London," Reggie said. He sat down and lay back staring at the sky.

"You come 'ere often?" Dick asked.

"No. I used to." Reggie paused. "With Dot, before we was married." He never spoke about his marriage, but he was suddenly filled with a desperate need to talk. He had been lonely for so long, scarcely even rowing with Dot, even when she upset and irritated him most, that |this proximity with a sympathetic person precipitated the words.

"Married?" Dick said, astonished. "You never said you was married." He felt almost betrayed. How could Reggie be married, if being married was like the perpetration of his experience tonight with Rose?

Reggie said slowly, "Everyone knows I'm married."

"Don't she ever go with you, then?" Dick asked.

"She don't go anywhere with me. We don't go anywhere together, 'cept bed." He put his hands under his head. "And I wouldn't go there if I could 'elp it."

"Why did you marry 'er, then?" Dick asked.

"God knows. We both wanted to then. 'Er Mum pushed us. Wanted to get Dot out of 'er 'ouse. It seemed all right."

"I don't ever want to get married," Dick said. Because Reggie had confided, and because it was so dark, he felt he could talk freely. He was ashamed of what he was saying but because he had only admitted it to himself before he felt intense relief in being able to confess. "I never kissed anyone till tonight. That tart Rose, she made me."

"Kissing's all right," Reggie said, "if you want to, but it's awful if you don't. I have to do more'n kiss Dot sometimes. I 'aven't for months, though."

"Why do you, if you don't want to?"

"Well, I'm married to 'er. She wants it. I got to."

Dick didn't like to think of Reggie making love. "I wouldn't," he said. "I couldn't."

"Once I get started it isn't so bad," Reggie said. "I never want to start."

They sat for a few minutes without speaking. Their confessions had had a cathartic effect and they felt a bond between them. Dick said, "I think there must be something wrong with me, not wanting girls, I mean, but not everyone wants sex, do they?"

"There's nothing wrong with you, mate," Reggie said comfortingly. "You're all right."

"It was terrible with Rose," Dick went on. "I felt sick; honest, it was disgusting."

"You don't dig 'er, that's all," Reggie said. "When you dig a chick, then you'll like it all right."

"I think I ought to get 'ome to Gran," Dick remembered. "It

33

was Grand-dad's funeral today and I'm supposed to be looking after 'er and all."

"Come on, then." Reggie stood up. "You going with Les tomorrow?"

"Are you?"

Reggie wanted to say no, I don't want to, but he didn't like to seem scared or priggish to Dick. "Yeah, I'm going."

"See you there, then," Dick said, looking forward to it.

"Let's 'ope the law keeps clear of us," Reggie said, then, in case he had sounded nervous, added, "I'd like to see 'em try anything on us, mate."

They felt tired as they climbed down to the road, their boots slipping on the steep dry earth. It was two o'clock and it would take them more than half an hour to reach home. Dick wished they hadn't come so far. They rode fast without attempting to speak. Dick held Reggie tightly and tried not to become sleepy. Suppose he fell asleep, even for a second? Once or twice he almost did, and when Reggie dropped him in the High Street, a few yards from Gran's house, he thought he could only just managed to walk there.

"See you tomorrow, mate," Reggie said, manoeuvring the bike in the middle of the road, and turning it.

" 'Night," called Dick.

Gran was awake when he unlocked the front door, and her voice called to him from the bedroom. She was lying in bed, the light on, the *Daily Mirror* on the pink paisley eiderdown.

" 'Allo, love," she said, "what 'ave you been up to?"

"I went for a ride on me mate's motor-bike," he said. "I forgot the time."

Gran's grey hair was in a fat plait which reached her shoulder. Dick didn't like it. It made him too aware of her age.

"Want anything to eat, duck?"

"No, I'm flaked out." He kissed her cheek. "See you in the morning, Gran."

She lay down. "Turn my light off, will you?"

Feeling mean, because he had obviously prevented her from sleeping, he turned off the switch.

Dick was in bed. The lamplight shone across the room and every now and then, when a car passed, the shadows moved up and across the ceiling. The bed was uncomfortable. The mattress was so thin and ridged that however he lay it dug into him.

Usually he was unaware of it but tonight, although he was very tired, he could not sleep. He even wished he was in his bed at home. That was a box spring divan which his parents had bought him for his sixteenth birthday. At the time he had considered it a mean present. He had wanted a suit. And they had reminded him of it continually during the year they paid for it.

"There's no cake, I'm afraid," his mother would say, if he asked for it. "We're paying off on your bed and we got to give up something."

He remembered this and thought it was better at Gran's, in spite of the mattress. For one thing, Gran didn't go on at him for being in late. She couldn't sleep when he was out but there were no recriminations.

He wasn't always so late as he had been tonight, anyway. Funny sort of day it had been, the funeral and then Rose and this ride with Reggie. He liked Reggie. He had never had a close friend, not even at school. He'd always been part of a group, never a leader, but a member of some gang or another. He'd never singled anyone out, or been singled out before. With Reggie he felt he was on the brink of real friendship. He liked him. He wanted to see him again. If Reggie stopped going to Nick's he thought he would want to stop going there too. He liked talking to him. Perhaps it was because their exchange had been so intimate, so soul-baring, that he felt this growing link.

Dot said, "Early, aren't you?" She was sitting up in bed reading an American comic, her only literature.

"Thought you'd be asleep," said Reggie. He was tired and didn't want an argument.

"Where you been?" Dot asked. "With a tart?"

"Of course I 'aven't," Reggie said wearily. "I was at Nick's."

"It closes at one. I'm not daft."

"I went for a ride on the bike."

"Yeah? Not by yourself."

"Oh, cut it," Reggie said. "I was with a bloke."

Dot threw her comic on to the end of the bed, stretched and yawned and lay down. "Well, let's get some sleep, for God's sake."

Reggie undressed and climbed into bed and pulled the light cord. Dot turned her back and after a few minutes he heard her breathing become louder and knew she was asleep. This is my married life, he thought. Half an hour in the morning before I

35

go to work, an hour for tea when I get in, and now. He suddenly longed for a proper home, where he would feel as happy as he had done in his parents' home before his mother had died. But how could he have a home? He couldn't even afford a flat. No one could be happy for ever in a stinking room in some bitch of a landlady's house. He thought of Dick and envied him. Dick hadn't spoken much about his grandmother's home, but enough to indicate that he was loved and welcomed and made comfortable. Dick hadn't dreaded going home tonight as he had. He would leave Dot, if only he had somewhere else to go. But now he could only find a similar room in a similar house, and at least Dot cooked his tea. He could go back to his father, he supposed. But he was pretty sure he had some woman who lodged in the same house, and probably wouldn't be overjoyed to have him back. He felt very alone, and yet not independent. He wasn't independent because he needed people. He didn't like to be on his own, he wanted love and he wanted friends. He only liked the gang because he could be part of it. He was greeted when he arrived. He was expected. He belonged. He wondered, as he listened to Dot's slight snoring, if he would ever marry again. He probably would, just because he didn't want to live alone. If I ever do, he thought, I'll make bloody sure I don't pick anyone like Dot. But how would he know? Dot was all right before they married. He didn't know then how their marriage would turn out, how it would deteriorate. He didn't really know how it had. He had gradually realized she didn't attract him physically any longer, made love to her less, become aware that she had other people to take that place, stayed away because he felt both guilty and disgusted, and now it was routine. He thought, if only I could go back two years and live them again. If only I could be sixteen now.

FIVE

GRAN said, "See 'oo's at the door, Dickie." It was Wednesday afternoon and they had had their dinner. Today the Meals on Wheels service had brought roast lamb and jam roll and Gran hadn't told them that Grand-dad had died so that Dick could eat his dinner. The smiling male welfare worker, harassed but determined not to show it, had run in from the van, the four plates with their metal covers piled on top of one another like the props of a juggler's act.

"Here you are, dear," he shouted to Gran. "Keeping your pecker up? Always got a smile, haven't you, not like some of the poor souls I see." He looked around, saw some plates waiting for him and neatly slid the dinners on to them. "Eat up, while it's hot, there's a good girl. Cheery-bye." He collected the two-and-eightpence Gran had been fumbling for in her purse, and ran out, closing the door behind him.

After Dick had washed up, scraping the remains of custard and gravy into the sink tidy, he had made tea and they had drunk three cups each, and talked about nothing in particular. Gran was just getting sleepy, and Dick was thinking he wouldn't mind half an hour himself, when there was a loud knock at the door, and Dick opened it and to his surprise saw his parents on the doorstep.

" 'Allo," he said, not pleased, "what you come for?" They didn't usually visit Gran more than once a month, but perhaps now they considered it a duty. Still, it wasn't like Dad to give up his half-day.

"We've come to talk to Mum," Dick's mother said. "We didn't 'ave much chance yesterday."

" 'Oo is it?" called out Gran. "Come in and don't stand nattering on the doorstep. I can't 'ear."

"It's us, Mum," Dick's mother called out, and she went into

37

the kitchen, taking off her black nylon gloves and putting them into her handbag as she did so.

" 'Allo, duck," said Gran. "This is a surprise."

"Well, we didn't 'ave a chance to get down to things yesterday, not really, so Fred and I thought we'd come and 'ave a chat this afternoon."

" 'Ave a cup of tea, then," Gran said. "Dick'll make a fresh pot. Put the kettle on, love," she said, as Dick and his father came in.

As soon as the tea was made and had brewed and they were all drinking, Dick's father coughed as if he were about to make a speech, blew his nose into a handkerchief with a maroon-and-green-striped border and said, "Joan and I've been thinking, Mum."

" 'Ave you?" said Gran sharply. "That's a change."

"We don't think it's right you should stay 'ere on your own," Dick's mother said.

"And where do you think I ought to be?" Gran asked.

"Well, I'm not going to beat about the bush," Dick's mother said. "You're an old woman and you ought to 'ave proper care."

"There's a very nice 'ome for elderly folk down our way," Dick's father said euphemistically. "You stand a good chance of getting in there. Joan 'ad a word with Dr. Woodside."

" 'E's not your doctor," Gran said. " 'E's mine."

"That's *why*," Dick's mother explained patiently, "that's why I went to see 'im. Because 'e knows all about you."

"And 'e said," Dick's father interrupted, "you'd go on the list and as soon as there's a place you'd be accepted."

"When someone's died to make room, you mean. I'd rather stay in me own 'ome," Gran said.

"Now listen, Mum," Dick's mother said firmly. "It's no good taking on that attitude. It's got to be gone into. It's for your own good. We're not trying to force you."

"What you trying to do then?" asked Gran.

"Just come and 'ave a look at the place," Dick's father said persuasively. "Arthur'll take us in the car."

"All got together, 'aven't you," Gran said. "You needn't 'ave wasted your breath. I'm staying put. The nurse'll come if I'm ill and I got the 'ome 'elp Tuesdays."

"There's your shopping," Dick's mother said, "and washing and cooking."

38

"I 'elp," said Dick.

"You?" His mother looked at him scornfully. " 'Ow long do you think you can stay off work?"

"Well, even if I worked I could do things when I got 'ome," Dick said.

"No one's going to rely on you. And since when 'as this been your 'ome?"

" 'E's welcome to make it is 'ome," Gran said.

" 'Is 'ome's with us," Dick's father ruled. "We like to know what 'e gets up to."

" 'E doesn't get into trouble 'ere," Gran defended him. "I brought you up all right. I can look after Dick."

"It's a different generation. You're too soft with 'im," Dick's mother argued.

"Gran wants me to stay," Dick said.

"I suppose it's all right temporary," Dick's mother answered, "until we get things settled."

There was a pregnant silence. Dick thought, I wish I could live on my own, with no one knowing where I am or caring what I do. For the moment he loathed them all, even Gran, because she was involved in this discussion.

Dad said, "Now, about this 'ome, Mum. You'll come and 'ave a look at it, won't you? You don't 'ave to decide."

"It's no good 'er dithering too long," said Dick's mother, "or she'll lose 'er chance."

" 'Ave a chat to the doctor about it," Dick's father urged.

"We can't be running over 'ere every five minutes you're ill," said Dick's mother.

"After all, you've paid your stamps long enough. You're entitled to be looked after."

"You're not taking charity, though. You give your pension and they give you a few shillings for your own bits and pieces, chocolate and that."

"There's a television."

"Arthur said 'e's free Saturday. Just to take you to 'ave a look."

"Well, I'll look," Gran said, "if it'll make you all 'appy. But I'm not staying. I'm staying 'ere."

Dick stayed with Gran until she went to bed at eleven. After his parents had left Gran had cried and said how awful it was being old, people tried to make up your mind for you as if you were a child. She said the family didn't want her; not that she'd live with any of them, even if they did, but it was dreadful the way her own children had no time for her. She and Dad had done everything for them and now they couldn't put her out of the way quickly enough. She'd heard about those Homes, thank you. Like prisons. If it wasn't for Dick she'd be really alone. He was the only one who bothered about her.

All the time she talked and cried Dick patted her shoulder and her hand and put his arm round her and was on edge to go out. He didn't want to miss tonight. They'd think he was chicken if he didn't go. When at last Gran went to bed, with a glass of hot milk and a generous tablespoon of medicinal whisky, he told her he was just going out for an hour to see some friends.

"We go up to the caff," he said, "we all meet there."

"Go and enjoy yourself," Gran said. "I'm 'alf asleep tonight. You won't keep me awake."

Before he left he changed his clothes, putting on his jeans and a dark sweater. He felt thrilled and afraid, hot and breathless with excitement. He closed the front door quietly behind him. He thought everyone in the road must be in bed. As he looked at the row of houses opposite the last square of lights popped into darkness and he heard a window being opened, squeaking upwards on its sash. The sound seemed remote and unreal, disconnected, no more than a sound effect in a radio play.

He walked quickly, the rubber soles of his shoes making almost no noise. His shadow stretched and dwindled between the lamplights. The plate-glass shop-front of the café, facing him as he turned the corner, shone like an illuminated cinema screen. The advertisements for Tizer and 7 Up and Coca-Cola made small dark geometrical shapes. Outside, on the pavement, were the boys, about ten of them. He recognized Les because he was taller and fatter than the rest, but Reggie, if he was there, was indistinguishable from the others. He approached them at a slower pace. He didn't want to look too eager. No one appeared enthusiastic. It would seem silly.

" 'Ere's Dick," said one of the boys. Dick picked out Reggie's parked bike. Then he saw Reggie. He grinned at him.

" 'Allo, mate."

" 'Allo," said Reggie.

"I suppose I got to say it all again," Les said aggressively.

"It's all right," said Reggie. "I'll give 'im the routine."

"Well, let's go." Les and four of the boys climbed into his car.

40

The others went over to the bikes.

"We're going up this school," Reggie explained. "The caretaker bloke's away and Les wants to do 'is place over, like 'e said. We're leaving the bike about an 'alf mile away, Les 'as told us all where to go. Then we're meeting up the school."

As Reggie started the bike, Dick asked, "Are we going to carve the 'ole 'ouse up?"

"Les don't do things by 'alf." Reggie remembered the janitor, who was a bad-tempered but not vindictive old man. He didn't really deserve Les's attention. It seemed to Reggie that it was cowardly to destroy when there was so little likelihood of being caught. A fight was all right. The other person had a chance. But this poor old sod couldn't protect anything. He wasn't even there.

Reggie and Dick were the last to leave. The other machines had driven off at short intervals. Now it was time to make for the particular point allotted them by Les. It was only five minutes away and they parked the bike in a small deserted car-park belonging to a public house.

"Seems a daft place to leave it," Reggie said. "It's the only thing 'ere. Anyone'd spot it."

"Les ought to know," Dick said. "I suppose it's safe enough."

They walked rapidly to the school building. Les was already there, and most of the other boys. The last one was approaching as Reggie and Dick joined the group.

"Now," Les said, "two of you keep a look out. Reggie, you go down there, and Bill on the other corner."

Although Reggie had been disapproving the whole episode he was disappointed that he wasn't going to take an active part. It wasn't any fun, hanging about in the street, waiting for cops that didn't come.

"The rest of us can get over the wall," Les said. "Someone give me a leg up."

The boy with the shaved head obliged and Les hoisted himself on to the wall, eased himself over the top and dropped down the other side. The sound of his feet thudding on to the playground asphalt seemed frighteningly loud. One by one they climbed over, and Reggie helped the last boy up. Then he walked to the corner of the building, which gave him the advantage of seeing in two directions.

Inside the playground the remaining boys gathered round Les.

"That's the shack, over there." He pointed to a small one-storey lodge with a flat roof which was attached to the main school building. Dick had never seen this school before but it gave him an uneasy sense of its authority. The windows were so large and unshuttered he couldn't believe that he wasn't being watched. The very feel of the playground underfoot brought back a timidity he had completely forgotten. He walked with the others, at each step putting his toe and then his heel to the ground to minimize sound. Les tried the lodge windows, but they were all shut.

"We'll 'ave to break one, then, won't we?" he said. He wrapped his hand in his handkerchief and plunged it through a small pane. They stood terrified, poised to run, as the glass shattered. Then, when nothing happened, no shout from Reggie or Bill, Les put his hand carefully through the broken pane, felt for the latch and opened the window. He put his hands on the sill and levered himself into the room.

Dick was the last to climb into the lodge. He wished he, and not Reggie, had been chosen to keep watch. Until he had climbed the wall he had been enjoying himself. Now he was really afraid. He was ashamed of himself for being afraid, and because of it, when he vaulted into the room he was the first person to begin the damage. He saw a carved oak clock on the mantelpiece, and with his whole arm swept it off the shelf and on to the floor. It was as if he had given a signal. At once the boys began to tear and break and smash and kick, going from one room to another. They ripped down the cotton curtains, pushed over tables, broke chairs, stamped on a wireless set, pulled down the pictures, emptied the drawers. When there was almost nothing left to harm, they climbed out into the playground again, and, reckless now, ran noisily to the wall. Les called to Reggie and he answered. No one had come near. Dick helped Les to climb the wall and was, in turn, helped by someone else. His feet stung as he dropped to the ground. The last boy had some difficulty in climbing by himself, and Reggie was lifted up and hung over the top so that the other boy could grasp his hands.

Dick thought, Supposing we're seen now. The few minutes extended in an agonized impatience.

At last they were all on the pavement. They were somehow sheepish. They felt flat. It was over. Their achievement gave no satisfaction. They said good night and walked away hurriedly in their different directions.

Reggie said, "It seemed like hours. What did you do?"

"Broke everything up," said Dick. "Smashed it all up."

" 'E'll get a fright when 'e opens 'is front door, then," Reggie said.

"I expect 'e'll get the law."

"They won't get us. No one could pin it on our lot. We wasn't seen."

"What's 'e like?" Dick asked. "The caretaker, I mean."

"Old Siddons? 'E was always getting 'is rag out at us. 'E's been there for donkey's years."

"Is 'e old, then?"

"Yeah," Reggie said. "They don't do that sort of work till they get the pension, do they?"

We shouldn't have done it, thought Dick. Suppose someone did Gran's home like we did tonight?

They didn't speak again until they reached the car-park and Reggie had wheeled the bike into the road.

"Les 'as got something else on for Sunday," Reggie said. "I'm cutting this one out, mate."

"Me too," said Dick. "I've 'ad enough for one week."

"What you doing Sunday?" Reggie asked.

"Nothing. Saturday I'm going out with Gran but I'm not doing nothing Sunday."

"Like to come on the bike, then, all day? We could go to Southend or somewhere."

"Wouldn't mind," said Dick.

Reggie added, "We could pick up a couple of birds. It's easy in those places, that's what they go for."

"Wouldn't mind," said Dick again. But it wouldn't have to be like Rose. He'd have to play it careful this time.

Reggie said to Dot, "I shan't be coming to your Mum's this Sunday." He had wanted to say it before but hadn't had the courage. Every Sunday, since they had married, excepting for three occasions when they had visited Reggie's father instead, they had spent the day with Dot's parents. For a long time he had wanted to break the routine, but each week he had nothing else to do. He had deliberately suggested to Dick that they spend this Sunday together.

Dot looked at him. "What you mean, not coming up to Mum's?"

"I'm busy this Sunday," Reggie said. "I'm going out on the bike with a friend."

43

"The same friend you went out with till three in the morning?"

"Yes."

"And you still try to kid me it's a bloke?"

"Of course it is."

"You wouldn't see a bloke that often."

"I 'aven't seen 'im that often."

Dot suddenly burst into tears. "You know what Mum'll think if we don't go there for dinner."

"If she thinks it, it's true. Why pretend we're still a couple of love birds when we're not? We don't go anywhere else together so why keep going up to your Mum's?"

"If we don't go up to Mum's we might as well not be married at all."

"Well, that's plain daft. What's that got to do with being married? Anyway, we might as well not be, the way we are."

" 'Oo's fault's that?"

"Not mine."

"Yes it is, leaving me alone night after night while you go up the caff."

"You find plenty to do."

"Only 'cause you don't do it."

Dot walked about the room as she spoke. For a long time she had been building up this grievance against Reggie. In her mind she had said to him many times "I'm leaving you" and "I'm getting out". But now the opportunity was here she didn't want to. She didn't love Reggie, but if they left each other she would be ashamed. It would look as if she couldn't hold him. Besides, there was the future. Where would she live? She couldn't face being with Mum and Dad again, and her five pounds and ten shillings a week as a grocer's shop assistant wouldn't be enough for her. Reggie earned good money. She liked to buy clothes. No, he'd married her and he was going to keep her. She said, "You don't do nothing any more. You can't expect me to go without. You don't even kiss me."

"I tell you why I don't," shouted Reggie. "Because I don't fancy you after God knows 'oo 'as been pawing you around."

"It's your fault. I'm not a nun."

"Too true." It wasn't his fault, it was all hers. She was a bloody tart, couldn't go without for more than a week.

"I suppose you expect me to wait till you feel like it."

"Yes, I do," Reggie said, "and this Sunday I don't feel like coming up to your Mum's neither. You can tell 'er what you like." He went out of the room and ran down the stairs so quickly that he was halfway down when the door he had pulled behind him slammed.

Dot stood crying in the middle of the room, between the two armchairs. She sat down on one of them and put her head on its worn arm. "Bloody cheek," she wept. "I'll pay 'im." Mum would half kill her if it came out. She'd blame her. She always did. Reggie couldn't do any wrong in Mum's eyes. The more she thought about it Dot realized she didn't want to leave Reggie. But by the way he'd spoken just now he could have left her already. How could she keep him? By getting pregnant. It was the only way. It wouldn't matter that it wasn't Reggie's baby. He'd know, but he couldn't prove it, he'd have to look after it. Perhaps she could even get him to make love tonight, if he came back, making it up. She'd be sorry and cry and he wouldn't be able to get out of it. And when John came round later she wouldn't wear anything. He always left it to her. That's why they liked married women, because it was easy and no complications. She didn't want a baby but it was better than letting Reggie go off with this other girl. What kind of a monkey did he think he was making of her, trying to kid her it was a bloke?

SIX

GRAN put on her black straw hat with its band of petersham
ribbon, stuck in a tortoiseshell hatpin with such ferocity that Dick
thought she would pierce her scalp, looked at the twelve-inch oak
replica of a grandfather clock and said, " 'E's late!"

"Only ten minutes," Dick said.

"Never mind 'ow long. I'm *going* to please 'im and 'e ought to
be 'ere prompt."

Almost as she spoke there came a rhythmic burst on a car
horn – tum-tiddly-um-tum, tum-tum.

"There 'e is," Dick said. "Come on, Gran."

She picked up her grey fabric gloves and started her slow walk
to the front door. Dick went behind her. Her coat came down
to her large mis-shapen ankles which spread out into black laced
shoes. Dick thought she looked as if she had no neck and no
thighs, a real Giles grandma.

Before they reached the front door Arthur's horn blared again.

"Can't 'e shut up," grumbled Gran, fiddling with the latch.
She opened the door. Arthur's car was parked directly in front
of the gate. Dick's mother was sitting in the back, so neat and
straight she was like a silhouette, done while you wait, in black
paper, on the promenade. Arthur leapt out of the car, hurried
round and opened the door for Gran.

"The carriage awaits," he said.

Gran eased herself in and Dick climbed into the back beside
his mother. Arthur bundled the ends of Gran's coat on to her
lap and slammed the door.

" 'Allo, Mum," said Dick's mother.

"I 'aven't changed me mind," Gran stated.

"Give the place a chance," Arthur said as he started the car.
"No good making up your mind before you see it."

"I don't care if it's Buckingham Palace," snapped Gran.

Dick's mother tch-tched and looked out of the window and

46

Dick saw she was tapping her fingers with irritation. He thought how pointless the outing was. He knew Gran would never live in this Home, however pleasant it turned out to be. She had been worrying about it all day. When he took her a morning cup of tea she had been wide awake, staring at the ceiling.

"They can't force me," she said, "they 'aven't got no law on their side, 'ave they?"

"Of course they 'aven't," Dick assured her. " 'Ow could there be a law about that?"

"I mean, if they said I was a trouble to them, or something like that?"

" 'Ow could they say that?" asked Dick. "You don't ask them for nothing."

"Suppose I get ill, though," Gran persisted, sitting up and putting in her teeth under the cover of her hand, "they could say I wasn't fit to be on me own."

"We'd find a way to keep you 'ere," Dick said. "Anyway, it wouldn't be an 'ome if you was really ill, it would be an 'ospital."

"I'm not going there either," said Gran as she drank her tea in long swills.

The Old People's Home consisted of two large Georgian terraced houses knocked together in a pleasant residential road. There were flights of steps up to both green front doors and Gran said, "I can't get up them for a start."

They stood in a group on the pavement.

Dick's mother said, "It's no good standing 'ere. This won't 'elp us." And she went up to one of the front doors and rang the bell.

Almost at once the door was opened and from where they stood they could see a woman in a white overall pointing and directing them to a side gate.

She came down the steps again and together they went through a tall gate set in the wall and into the grounds of the Home. Five old men sat on two iron seats puffing at pipes and meditating. The house, which had a basement area in front, sloped up at the back to garden level, and through the big ground-floor windows they could see tea already being prepared. Two half slices of bread and a small cake in a paper cup were being placed on each thick white plate. There were tea-cups and saucers piled on a trolley and on a table were about ten unopened cans of butter beans. They walked past the windows, staring in.

47

"I 'ope they give the poor buggers more than that," Gran said sharply. Dick's mother sighed.

The back door was open and the white-coated woman was there to meet them.

"Come along in," she said, and took Gran's elbow in a proprietary manner. They followed her into a wide entrance hall at the front of the house. On one side were double doors and the word LOUNGE was written across them, three letters on each door.

"This way," said the woman who had introduced herself as the secretary, Miss Sussman. She had a long sallow face and dark brown hair pinned up on her head.

The lounge was furnished with cretonne-covered chairs and sofas, and several small tables. At the far end one of the earliest television sets was switched on and a number of old women were watching the afternoon's sport. One of them had fallen asleep. Two more were knitting and a further couple were having an animated conversation on a sofa. Another, by herself, very small and spry in an orange dress, was tearing up pieces of printed paper.

"Now then, Granny Hopkins," said Miss Sussman, "what's going on?" She went over to her and removed the papers. "That's Granny Wilson's church magazine and you've no right to destroy it."

"Muck!" said Granny Hopkins fiercely. "Rubbish!"

Miss Sussman spoke to her severely and Granny Hopkins turned her back and stared sulkily out of the window.

"Let me show you the bedrooms," Miss Sussman said. "We've a lift here to help those poor old legs."

The lift was modern and the door opened and closed automatically. Dick could see Gran was nervous of it and was making it yet another reason not to come here. The lift stopped and the door slid open. Miss Sussman, who had not relinquished her hold on Gran's elbow, guided her on to the landing.

"Don't worry about slipping, dear. I know it looks shiny but we have a non-slip plastic seal on our floors." She took them into a bedroom.

"Lovely, isn't it?" said Dick's mother.

"We're rather proud of it ourselves," Miss Sussman agreed.

There were five beds in this big, airy room, and cubicle curtains of a blue, red and orange Jacobean design. Each cubicle had a chest of drawers and a chair.

"We never have more than five to a room," Miss Sussman said.

"*Five*," muttered Gran.

"Next door is the Cherry Room," Miss Sussman said, taking them there. "All our rooms are named after fruit or flowers."

She opened the door with a flourish, to reveal an old woman in a vest with sleeves and a pair of black bloomers which reached to her knees.

"Oh, Granny Wilberstone," Miss Sussman said, "why didn't you draw your cubicle curtains if you were going to change?"

"Didn't expect visitors," said Granny Wilberstone spiritedly.

"Well, never mind this time." Miss Sussman withdrew on to the landing again and they backed out with her. "Come, I'll show you the bathroom."

Again there were cubicle curtains, this time of yellow transparent plastic between a number of washbasins. Two doors, marked BATH and TOILET, led off. Miss Sussman opened the bath door and then closed it, allowing them a second's glimpse of a bath raised on taloned feet.

The main door opened and Granny Wilberstone shuffled in, now wearing an overall and a pair of carpet slippers. She held a second pair of bloomers in her hand.

"Can't go anywhere today," she said, glittering malevolently. She pushed past Dick's mother to a washbasin, filled it with water and some soap powder from a container on a shelf and plunged the bloomers in.

"That's the second time today," Miss Sussman said. "You must remember to ask Doctor for some more pills." She turned to Dick's mother. "We have excellent medical attention. Matron is a qualified Sister and Doctor calls every day. We know old people have plenty of aches and pains." She paused and thought. "A chaplain calls every Sunday. Visiting times are Wednesday afternoons and Saturdays and Sundays." She smiled round. "Any questions?"

They shook their heads.

"Cook is a qualified dietician." Dick thought of the tea he had seen through the kitchen windows. "We can't have too many fads and fancies as I'm sure you'll understand, but within reason no one has to eat anything she really dislikes. The men live in the next-door house and eat separately, but we have plenty of get-togethers." She smiled archly. "We've even had a romance. One of our favourite grannies met her Mr. Right at a housie-housie evening."

"What about the telly?" asked Arthur.

"They can watch it whenever they like. We only have the B.B.C. on our set – we're dependent on charity for our luxuries, you see. But I think it's a good thing. It stops a lot of bickering."

As they trooped out of the garden gate Arthur said, "There you are, Mum, you might even find yourself a boy-friend."

"It's ever so nice, isn't it," said Dick's mother. "I'm sure you'll be 'appy."

"Blimey," Gran said, "I'd rather be dead than go there, sleeping in a room with a lot of dirty women 'oo wet their knickers. No thank you very much."

They argued with her all the way home, but Gran was adamant.

"Very well," said Dick's mother tightly. "If you can manage on your pension, well and good. But don't come to us. We've done all we can."

"I wouldn't come to you if I was starving," Gran said.

"Well you wouldn't get charity if you did, not after this."

"Joan don't mean it," Arthur said. "We're just all a bit disappointed. We were set on your going there."

"For your own good," said Dick's mother.

"You can all mind your own business," Gran said. "I can look after myself."

"You won't always be able to, you know," said Dick's mother. "You'll be sorry one day."

Gran forked a pickled onion on to her plate. "It isn't going to be easy. Dad didn't eat that much and it was two pounds a week more." She looked at the onion reflectively. "I won't be able to buy them bits and pieces I fancy."

"Yes you will," Dick said. "I'll get work up 'ere and live with you. Then I can pay you for 'aving me."

"Do you mean it? Will you really? Then they couldn't make me go to that place, could they?" Gran's relief was so intense, her gratitude so overwhelming, that her cheeks and neck flushed red.

" 'Course I do. I'll go and see about working on Monday, first thing."

He was happy he had made the decision. He would stay permanently with Gran. It was, he realized, what he wanted. His parents were like strangers. Today he had seen his mother objectively. He was quite separate from them and their way of living. He didn't really like them, certainly didn't love them. He loved Gran. He was happy here. He liked the friends he had made, or at least he liked Reggie. He was looking forward to going out with Reggie tomorrow. He had better go to the café tonight and fix the time to meet in the morning. He hoped it was going to be a fine day.

He waited until Gran had gone to bed before he went out. She wanted to talk to him about her money worries, about illness, about the Old People's Home and countless smaller problems. Before there had been Grand-dad, almost totally deaf in the last year, but nevertheless a kind of audience. Dick half listened, said yes and no at the necessary places and enjoyed his own thoughts. He didn't begrudge Gran his company. As long as he could go out later he was content to sit and drink tea now. But at eleven, with Gran snoring, he was almost nervously anxious to be out of the dilapidated and stuffy house. He changed into a pair of tight black jeans and his fingers shook and slipped as he fastened the buckle of the wide belt. He ran down the road experiencing an odd internal excitement, a tingling in his throat and stomach. Seeing the lighted café and Reggie's bike and Les's car his mood was almost one of bliss. He felt he belonged. He wasn't going away from here. He was part of his environment.

Les looked up from his glass as Dick entered. Two tables had been pulled together and the boys, Reggie amongst them, were sitting round. Dick went to the counter, bought himself a Coca-Cola and sat down too. He said happily, "I'm going to stay with me Gran for good now. I'm going up the labour exchange Monday."

"What for?" Les asked in his slow, slightly menacing voice.

"For work of course."

"Work?"

"Yes, to give Gran some money. She can't manage without."

"You come at the right moment," Les said. "We've just been 'aving a little talk about money."

Dick looked at him, already half understanding.

" 'Ow about me joining in, then?"

"Depends if you're chicken or not."

"I'm not chicken, mate, not over nothing."

"You don't need to be."

Reggie said, "We 'aven't said we're doing it yet, Les."

"Don't tell me, will you?" said Dick.

"Well." Les put both his arms on the table. "What we've been doing is kid's stuff. I mean what do you get out of it 'cept kicks. I mean nothing real. Take old Siddons's 'ouse. 'E 'ad it coming but it didn't do nothing for us. There was nothing there worth 'aving. Nothing to flog after, I mean. What we want to do is little shops. Little shops and cinemas. You can get a packet out of doing cinemas. A friend of mine done some cinemas." He inhaled deeply. "We're bright boys, you know. If we work together like, we're in the money."

"It's real," said Shaved Head.

"I'll let you know Monday," Reggie said. "I don't fancy ending up inside." He thought, I don't want to do it. I earn enough for Dot and me. One didn't want to embark on criminal life. It was all Dot's fault. If she were decent he would be at home with her now. Obliquely he blamed her for Les's suggestion. He wondered how Dick felt about it. But Dick needed money for his grandmother. He had just said so. He would talk to Dick about it tomorrow.

Reggie woke up at half past eight. Dot was still asleep so he got up and put the kettle on for tea. It was a whistling kettle and the whistle woke Dot. She opened her eyes and blinked and closed them again.

"What's the time?"

" 'Alf eight."

" 'Alf eight," Dot echoed.

"I'm going out. Forgotten?" He thought, now there's going to be another row. But Dot didn't answer him, and he made the tea and then drank it. Then he washed the cups under the cold tap, emptied the tea-leaves into a rusty metal sink tidy, swilled the sink round and filled it up to wash himself.

Dot said suddenly and quietly, "You'll 'ave to stop going with this girl."

Reggie was about to deny it was a girl when he decided not to. "Why?" he said.

"Because I'm 'aving a baby." She didn't know if it was true, but it might be. She hadn't succeeded in getting Reggie to make love, but she hadn't taken any precautions with John for the last two nights.

"If you are, it's not mine," Reggie said. "That don't give you anything on me."

Dot was at once terribly frightened. Why had she said it? Why had she done it? Suppose Reggie had been telling the truth and it was a bloke he'd been seeing. Now she had told him straight out she had other men.

"No one can prove it's not yours."

"Yes, they can," Reggie answered, remembering dimly something he'd read in the paper. "There's blood tests. I 'aven't made love to you for three months."

Dot began to cry hysterically. "I made it up, Reggie, honest. I'm not 'aving any baby." But all the time she thought, suppose I am. She shouted at him, "It's your fault if I am, leaving me alone."

"Look," Reggie said, his voice quite controlled. "We've said all this before. If our marrying was a mistake, per'aps we'd better pack it in. If you're 'aving someone else's baby you needn't think I'm going to pretend I'm its father. If you are, we're finished." All the time he was speaking he was thinking, have I been unkind, have I not done all I could for her? He looked at her in her rather grubby but elaborate nightdress. Her emerging feet weren't very clean. Yesterday's make-up was still on her face. Little crusts of sand, dirtied by mascara, were visible in the corners of her eyes. He could never kiss her again. However desperately she wanted him, however necessary to mend their marriage, he couldn't.

Dot came over to him and put her arms round him. "Reggie, don't leave me. I don't want to be alone." Her tears wetted his vest.

"I don't know," he said. " 'Ow can we go on like this?"

She pulled away from him. "You bloody sod!" she screamed. "You don't care about anyone 'cept yourself. I 'ate you! I don't know what I ever saw in you. You're nothing."

Reggie turned his back and dressed quickly. Then, without looking at her again, he went out, closed the door and ran downstairs.

That's that, he thought. And wheeled his bike out into the road and went to meet Dick.

SEVEN

Even at nine o'clock it was hot enough to ride the bike without wearing jackets.

"It's going to be a scorcher," Reggie shouted. "We'll 'ave to 'ire bathing trunks and 'ave a swim."

The road, almost empty, radiated a haze. There was an atmosphere of dryness and dust. Curtains were drawn in the serried rows of semi-detached and terraced houses. Sunday papers protruded like tongues from the letter-boxes. They passed paper boys and milk roundsmen, moving at snail's pace on their bicycles and floats, or so it seemed to them as they raced along the streets.

"What time will we get there?" Dick asked. This was Reggie's outing. He knew exactly where they were going, how they were going to spend their day.

"Not long. Another forty minutes." That was the joy of a bike, nothing really held you up. At traffic lights you were the first away, in traffic jams you threaded your way to the top of the queue and then left it behind you. Dick, more blasé than when he first rode pillion, didn't hold on to Reggie now. One hand on the saddle, one free, he looked about him, the world shaded through the goggles Reggie had lent him, his hair blowing behind his ears.

The first glimpse of the sea came unexpectedly. One moment they were cruising through the town, the next they were on the front, with white railings along the promenade and the beach, wet and wide, a mile of it, before the blue and white lines of the sea.

Reggie slowed and stopped. They took off their goggles and everything was suddenly vivid and almost hurt their eyes.

"Smashing," said Reggie. "Isn't it?"

The pier, far along the sands, was quite out of the sea. Down at the water's edge one or two matchstick figures were bathing

54

A dog ran barking along the beach, kicking up sand, digging his nose in it, running on again, enjoying it to a point of dottiness.

"Let's get something to eat," Reggie said, "I'm empty."

They parked the bike and walked along the promenade but all the beach cafés were closed.

"We'll 'ave to try the town then," Reggie said. "D'you want to walk or shall we go back for the bike?"

"Walk," Dick said. He was suddenly aware how lovely the fresh air was. He had had only one seaside holiday in his life and that had been the summer when he was twelve. It hadn't been much fun. He remembered wet days and his mother nagging and being forced to sit on the windy sands and bathe when he didn't want to. He hadn't wanted to go the next year and had gone to stay with Gran while his parents, together with another couple, holidayed at Skegness. After that there had been no more summer holidays. Dick supposed, now, that money must have been shorter, or perhaps, because he had been growing up, his clothes had cost more. Anyway, about that time his parents had become discontented with their home and the hire-purchasing era had begun. He had nearly taken a holiday last year. He had saved enough and decided to go to a holiday camp. But when he finally applied he was told that the camp was fully booked, that he would have to book in December if he wanted to go in August. So he bought himself a new suit instead. Afterwards he was glad. His suit was very smart and he thought he got more pleasure from wearing it than he would have from the holiday.

Reggie said, "Funny 'ow 'ungry you get, riding."

Dick nodded. "I'm starving." He pointed to a café on the street corner, illuminated even in the bright sunlight. OPEN ALL DAY it said in blue strip lighting. The words HOT SNACKS flashed on and off and oranges bobbed on top of a revolving flask of orange drink. "There, Reggie. Let's go in there."

They ordered tea and bread-and-butter and bacon-and-eggs. The butter was margarine, they thought, and the eggs were spotted with bits left in the much-used frying fat. The bacon wasn't crisp enough and the tea was weak.

"Blimey," Reggie said, "they'd better not try and skin us on this lot." But they were hungry and ate with enjoyment. They paid the bill and walked out into the street again. Other people were out by this time – women in beige and pink pull-on felt hats and fitted coats, on their way to a nearby church, and small children and their mother in trousers hurrying to the beach.

"Where are we going?" Dick asked.

"The amusement arcade." Reggie walked slightly ahead of Dick, leading the way.

It was lit, too, very brightly, and a record was playing loudly. Two middle-aged men in striped blue suits and no ties were pulling out the handles of the pin tables. Both men had sideboards and unshaven faces. The music was punctuated by the plop of the balls hitting the stops on the pin tables, and the twang of the starting handle.

"Too early for birds," Reggie said. "We'll 'ave to 'ang on for an hour." He felt in his pocket for pennies, found some and went over to one of the tables. The lights flashed, the ball rebounded and bounced on. The numbers mounted, didn't reach the total required for a refund, the ball disappeared and the lights went out.

Reggie put in another penny.

Dick could see the sunlight outside. He would have liked to go on the sands. He put a penny into a slot where Esmeralda, a glowering waxen head with head-scarf and ear-rings, told the future. The little card, the size of a bus-ticket, shot out, and told him that he had a happy month ahead, with the chance of financial increase and romance. This last would follow a slight setback. His lucky colour was blue.

The financial increase might be this job Les was talking about. But romance wasn't in his line. He showed the card to Reggie.

"That's the bird you're going to pick up today."

Dick didn't want to pick up any girls. He knew Reggie wanted to and didn't want to spoil Reggie's fun. But he felt at ease and happy with Reggie and didn't want the strain and boredom of making conversation. On the other hand he might find a girl he liked. He felt that somewhere there must be a girl who attracted him.

As Reggie had said it would, the amusement arcade began to fill up at eleven o'clock. At about twenty past, two girls came in. They wore cotton dresses and white cardigans and white sandals and their painted big-toe nails emerged at the tops, slightly longer than the soles of their shoes. Reggie nudged Dick. "They'll do." He sauntered over and stood behind the girls and Dick followed. The girls giggled and talked to each other self-consciously, and put a penny into a machine where two wooden figures in striped

56

jumpers and white shorts kicked a ball in response to frantic handle-turning. The two girls turned the handles. One managed to score a goal and the penny was returned.

"One nil for Arsenal," said Reggie. The girls giggled. "Go on, make it a draw."

"We run out of pennies," said the taller and mousier girl.

"Thought you females always kept a penny in case." More giggles. " 'Ere you are, 'ave this one on me," Reggie handed the girl a penny. "I'll play you."

Reggie took one handle, the girl the other. The blonde girl came and stood by Dick. They had paired off.

Dick looked at the girl who was his. She was rather fat but he supposed quite pretty. People always said blondes were the best, so he was lucky.

Reggie's girl shrieked out. She had won her match with him. Reggie said, "You girls on your own, then?" They nodded. "Come and 'ave a drink with us, then."

"Thanks very much," Dick's girl said with affected formality.

They left the pin tables and walked in two's towards the front.

"There's a pub on the corner," Reggie said.

"That's right."

"You live 'ere, then?"

"That's right."

Dick felt he must make conversation too.

"What's your name?" he asked the girl.

"June. What's yours?"

"Dick."

"Mine's Brenda," said Reggie's girl over her shoulder.

"You just down for the day?" asked June.

They talked stiltedly until they reached the public house. Reggie held open the door of the saloon bar and they all went in and sat down at a round table with an Ind Coope's ashtray in the middle.

"What's it going to be?" asked Reggie.

Without hesitation the girls asked for gin-an-orange, and Reggie and Dick ordered pints of brown ale. Dick wished that the girls hadn't come to the amusement arcade. Then Reggie might have given up the idea.

'We thought of 'iring costumes and bathing," Reggie said.

"You can get them at the changing places," June said. "We could go 'ome and get ours."

They arranged to meet after dinner. Reggie and Dick went back to the café where they had had breakfast and ate meat pies and jam roll and drank cups of tea. Then they hurried down to the pier entrance where they had arranged to meet Brenda and June. The girls hadn't arrived and Dick began to hope that they had picked up some other boys or simply changed their minds. But just as he was about to suggest it to Reggie an arm slipped into his and June's voice said, "I bet you thought we was lost."

"We knew you couldn't forget us," Reggie said.

"Go on. Listen to 'im. 'Oo does 'e think 'e is?"

"Fancies 'imself, doesn't 'e?"

"Come on." Dick interrupted, almost rudely. "Show us where we get the bathing things."

They walked arm in arm to the big changing pavilion on the promenade.

"Sorry we can't go in there with you," Reggie called, as June and Brenda went through the door marked LADIES. He and Dick went into the half of the building reserved for men, put sixpence each into a slot on the turnstile and walked the length of the wet wooden slatted floor. A woman in an overall fetched two pairs of black swimming trunks and showed them into a small cubicle. They changed into the ill-fitting trunks, hung their clothes on hooks, locked the cubicle door and went out, barefoot, to the promenade. As they walked Reggie hung the cubicle key on his wrist.

The girls were waiting for them, self-conscious in tight bathing suits, Brenda's a pink satin bikini revealing three large moles on her back, and June's a kind of ruched cotton with a floral design. Reggie whistled. The girls giggled. Dick thought how hairy June's legs were, fine blonde hair on rough red skin. They ran down the beach, off the hot promenade on to the hot sand into the cold sea. The girls screamed and splashed and floundered. Dick and Reggie swam quite strongly. Dick said, spitting out water, "I 'aven't been swimming since school."

"Don't you never go up to the baths now, then?"

"No. Never."

They stopped swimming and trod water, looking back at the girls.

"We'd better go to 'em," Reggie said. He swam back, then, when he was in his depth again, walked. Brenda came close to him, put both hands into the sea, palms outwards, and splashed water at him. Reggie caught hold of her and she screamed. He tried to duck her and she clung to him, loving this game in which he was strong and she was helpless.

Dick felt he should be doing the same and plunged at June. They shrieked and laughed and fought, and then, exhausted, came out of the sea and lay down on the sand to dry. The sun pricked their skins, made red patterns through their closed eyelids. Brenda moved closer to Reggie so that their legs touched and put her cheek against his shoulder.

He was suddenly reminded of Dot. He'd completely forgotten her during the morning but now, as Brenda touched him, he thought of her and how like her Brenda was. He didn't want her, he didn't want either of them. He felt an intense repugnance at the warmth and tickling sensations of Brenda's body. Dot was enough for him. Why had he picked up this tart, out on her Sunday routine? Why get tied up with a couple of stupid birds when he and Dick could have spent a quiet, pleasant day on their own? It was an effort to be with girls. You had to talk and flirt and neck, even if you didn't feel like it. He had thought that after these months of not making love to Dot he would be all ready to do it with someone else. Well, he wasn't. He didn't have the slightest urge. She might have been Dot for all the passion she aroused. He stood up and said, "I'm going to get dressed."

"Whatever for?" asked Brenda crossly. "Don't you want to go in the water again?"

"No. I 'ad enough of it. You coming?"

"Yes," Dick said, standing up too. "I feel too 'ot. I don't want to get covered in blisters."

"I suppose we'd better come too, then," grumbled June.

They walked silently up the beach, across the burning asphalt of the promenade and into the changing rooms. It seemed dank and gloomy after the sunlight. The boys unlocked their cubicle which smelt of seawater, and mildew. They took off their still wet trunks and slapped them on to the floor.

" 'Ow do you feel about them two?" Reggie asked, rubbing his shoulders with the small hired towel.

" 'Ow do you?" Dick asked warily.

"I've 'ad enough of them."

"So 'ave I, mate." Dick put on his vest and his voice came through it. "Shall we dump 'em then?"

"Can't be quick enough for me."

"What shall we do after? Do you want to bathe again."

"No," Reggie said. "I don't want to do nothing. Just sit in

the sun and not 'ave to listen to those birds yapping is all I want."

"Okay." Dick buckled his belt, picking up the bathing trunks and towels in one hand and unlocked the door with the other. They were ready before the girls this time.

"Shall we wait?" Dick asked.

"No." Reggie said. "Let's go." They began to run as fast as they could along the promenade, then jumped the three-foot wall on to the beach. The tide was coming in and the narrowing stretch of sand was crowded with deckchairs and windbreaks and digging children. Reggie slowed down. "They couldn't spot us now. I bet they're mad at us."

"I'd like to see their faces," Dick said, grinning. He felt malicious towards the girls. They had spoilt what should have been a wonderful day.

"There's a couple of chairs," Reggie pointed out. In a row of seated people were two empty deckchairs with faded orange canvas and brown varnished frames. They sat down, leaned back and closed their eyes. For a while neither of them spoke, then Reggie said, "What do you think about this lark of Les's?"

"I want to do it," Dick said. "I want the lolly for Gran. Otherwise she'll get put in one of those 'omes."

"I suppose I could do with it too," Reggie said. If Dick had decided against it, then he would have agreed. He felt drawn towards Dick today. Dick was his only friend. After his final, and it *was* final, row with Dot he was quite alone and without emotional relationships. He needed someone to talk to, someone to take the place which had first belonged to his mother, briefly to his father and then to Dot.

"I'm on me own now," he said abruptly. "I'm not going back to Dot."

"Where you going then?" Dick was so surprised he didn't know what to say.

"I don't know, but not back there, 'cept for me things."

"What you left 'er for?" Dick asked.

"I don't even like 'er. Now she tells me she's 'aving a kid, and it's not mine, so I'm getting out. Fast."

Dick said, "I'm glad I never got caught up with one. Sometimes I think I'd like to, but when you tell me what 'appens I think I'm lucky."

A ticket collector came and stood in front of them.

"Shilling, please."

"We're not *buying* 'em," Reggie said. "Anyway, we was just going."

"Too bad," answered the ticket man, unsmilingly. "You'll 'ave to pay just the same."

Dick gave the man two sixpences. "We 'ad better go, 'adn't we, Reggie, if we're going to see Les tonight?"

"I'm not in an 'urry," Reggie said. "I got nowhere to go really."

"I forgot," Dick said. "Where you going to 'ave tea then?"

"I'll eat something at Nick's later."

"Where you going to live?"

"Find a room, I suppose. My Dad might let me sleep up at 'is place for a night or two."

Dick thought, I don't suppose Gran would mind if he spent the night at home. "I'll ask me Gran if you can stop with us," he said.

"Do you think she'd mind?" asked Reggie hopefully. He didn't really want to go to Dad's. It would mean telling him about Dot.

"Gran's easy," Dick said. He was quite excited at the thought of Reggie staying. Suddenly he felt possessive about Reggie. He was his friend. They did things together, like today, and like this job Les had for them. He was very happy.

"Want an ice?" he asked.

"Wouldn't mind." They left their deckchairs and went to the yellow kiosk on the promenade.

"What you want?" said Dick. They decided on tubs and Dick paid. "It's been a smashing day," he said.

"We'll come again some time," said Reggie.

"Well?" asked Les.

"Count us in, Les."

"We got to case the joint first. You better come with me tomorrow night."

Reggie raised both his thumbs to show that without doubt they would be there.

"Meet you 'ere, then, about eleven." They were at Nick's.

"See you, mate."

Reggie and Dick finished their drinks and went out to the bike.

"I'm tired," Reggie said.

"So am I. We started early this morning."

"Will your Gran be in bed?"

"Snoring 'er 'ead off."

"I wonder if Dot thinks I'm coming back."

"She'll find out, won't she?"

Reggie felt lonely and depressed. What a mess life was.

Dick drew the curtains back and opened the window. Reggie was already in bed. In the faint light his dark hair was like soot smudged on the pillow. His features weren't discernible.

Dick crossed the room to the bed and climbed in. Alone he had stretched across it, now almost self-consciously he kept to his own half. He had never shared a bed before.

"Good night," he said.

"Good night," answered Reggie.

Dick lay quietly on his back without moving. After a few minutes the desire to turn on his right side became irresistible. It was the way he always went to sleep. He turned towards the centre of the bed and his shoulder came into contact with Reggie's arm. Reggie lay perfectly still. He could feel the warmth of Dick's body close to him and curiously he could feel his own heart begin to thump a little and his breathing become irregular. He found Dick's closeness more disturbing than he had found Dot for a long time.

Dick felt Reggie's arm, hard and muscular, pushing into his shoulder. It was uncomfortable almost, yet he did not move away. There was something satisfying in the contact with somebody with whom he felt friendship. It was reassuring to know that somebody to whom he could talk without restraint, with whom he had shared the day, was there next to him, warm, breathing, as distinct from being with him in the café, on a beach, on a bike. There was nothing between them any more, not furniture not clothes, it was dark and they were close and it was reassuring.

Reggie tried to control his breathing but his heart continued to thump and he felt a trembling inside him which he could not stop even by tensing his stomach muscles. Why? he thought to himself, why do I feel like this? It's only Dick there, not a girl. But he liked Dick very much. Dick was a straightforward bloke. You could talk to him and he understood and you could trust him. Yes, he liked Dick a lot. He felt an impulse to put his arm round Dick's shoulder. Without Dick where would he be tonight?

Dick was getting rather drowsy, then deliberately, as if they had been walking along the promenade together, Reggie turned towards him and stretched out his arm, only now they weren't walking side by side, they were lying face to face.

Dick moved too, spontaneously reacting to Reggie's affectionate movement. Each felt the other's breath against his face, the other's arm around him.

Quite without deliberation, without intention, without thought, they held each other closely and then they kissed.

EIGHT

WHEN Reggie woke up the sun was shining through the cotton curtains almost obliterating the pattern. For a moment he couldn't think where he was. On a few occasions he had woken up in a strange bedroom, after a party or a fight. He moved and as he did so felt the warmth of Dick's body beside him and he remembered. He lay there, his eyes open, staring at the discoloured ceiling. His thoughts kaleidoscoped: his row with Dot, last night here, in bed, with Dick, then back to Dot again, and he had a visual image of their room and of her in their bed against the wall. He was almost dreaming. Suddenly, completely awake and with a start, he sat up, so brusquely that he jerked the sheet away from Dick and woke him.

Dick opened his eyes, closed them, opened them again and looked at Reggie. Reggie smiled and glanced at his wrist-watch.

"I got to go to work," he said. He had turned his head so that he did not meet Dick's eye.

"Do you want some breakfast?" Dick asked.

"No, thanks. I'll get a cup of tea at the garage." Still without looking at Dick, he swung his legs over the edge of the bed and sat for a minute stretching. Then he reached for his clothes which hung over the brass foot of the bed, pulled them towards him and started to dress.

Dick watched him. He had never made love before and he felt a sense of warm contentment and gratitude and affection for Reggie. He longed to put his hand on Reggie's arm. He looked at Reggie's arms, strong and muscular, the shoulders cut by the narrow curve of his white vest, the springing metal watch strap on one wrist, the small golden hairs on the forearms and hands. The desire to touch him was almost overwhelming but he didn't dare and instead turned his head away on to the pillow. He felt Reggie stand up and heard him moving about the room. He wanted to talk to him, the words were in his mind and several times

64

he almost said them, but each time Reggie's lack of response, his apparent indifference, stopped him. Reggie combed his hair and put on his jacket.

"I'll 'ave a wash downstairs," he said. "Then I'd better get going."

He paused by the bed and Dick's heart seemed to swerve. He's going to kiss me, he thought. Let him kiss me. But Reggie went to the door and Dick shut his eyes and swallowed.

"Cheerybye," said Reggie.

"So long," said Dick, and he listened as Reggie went quietly downstairs so as not to waken Gran, and heard the tap running into the sink and the faint sound of the cistern flushing outside. He lay in bed as close to the point of crying as he had been since he was a child. Perhaps Reggie might come upstairs before he left, he thought. He must want to speak about it too. But in a matter of moments he heard the door latch and the motor-bike start and the diminishing roar took Reggie away from him for the day. It might be for more than the day. Neither had spoken of more than one night yesterday, when Dick had suggested that Reggie should stay. Reggie might not come back at all. He might never refer to last night or resume even the intimacy of their friendship. He thought he would want to die if that happened. He thought he would have to force Reggie to talk to him, wait for a moment when he could be alone with him and ask him why he had left this morning without a relevant word.

He got up and dressed and went down to make Gran her cup of tea. He hadn't told Gran that Reggie had spent the night in the house. She had been asleep when they came home for tea, snoring in the chair by the unlit fire. Quietly he had taken bread and cheese from the larder and tiptoed out again. When they had come in late Gran had been asleep again, in bed. Dick knew she wouldn't mind. He wanted to ask her if she would let Reggie stay there for always but with a kind of superstition he felt that if he did Reggie would never return. It would be tempting providence.

"My mate came back with me last night," he said, sitting on the edge of her bed. " 'E 'ad nowhere to go."

"Not in trouble is 'e?" asked Gran.

"Not that sort of trouble. Only with 'is wife."

"That's all right, then. I don't mind that."

"We went to the seaside," Dick said. He wanted to talk about Reggie and the things they had done together.

"That's nice," said Gran. "It was ever so 'ot in 'ere. Did you bathe?"

"Yes, we 'ired costumes." Dick finished his tea. "It was smashing there. I thought it was smashing."

He didn't like to think of Reggie in the sea. He remembered him clearly, playing with Brenda, hugging her, holding her, pulling her, as close together as if they had been in bed. It was daft, he knew. It never helped to be jealous. But he was, and it was even worse because last night probably meant nothing to Reggie. He was just randy. Men did do things with other men when they were randy, everyone knew that. It didn't mean they felt anything special though.

The tobacconist's shop was in Streatham. It was small and on a corner and the window facing one street displayed cigarettes and pipes and tobaccos and one or two lighters. The other window, slightly smaller, was filled with sweets of a cheap variety, nothing over tenpence a quarter, plenty of sherbet and gobstoppers and chewing gum and chocolate bars. In the daytime papers and magazines were suspended from a frame attached to the door lintel. Weekly papers such as *Red Star*, and *Red Letter* and *Lucky Star* predominated. Les stood with Dick and Reggie and the boy with the shaved head outside the coffee bar on the opposite corner. It was a quarter to twelve and the coffee bar was about to close. Groups of teenagers, less menacing in appearance than the crowd at Nick's, were beginning to surround Les and his group. They wore blazers and one had a long London University scarf hanging round his neck. The ends came to his knees. They split into twos and threes and calling good night walked away in different directions. The coffee-bar owner came and closed and locked the door.

"Come on," Les said. "We can't stand 'ere." They went over to where Les's car and Reggie's bike were parked at the kerb.

"We seen the place," Les said. "We 'ad a good look. Let's go to my 'ome. We'll talk it over there." He got into his car and Shaved Head sat beside him and he drove away quite fast.

" 'Ang on," Reggie said to Dick. Dick put his hands in the pockets of Reggie's jacket and leaned against his back. It's different now, he thought. Every time I touch him now it's different. Had Reggie planned it? he asked himself for the hundredth time. It was almost a traumatic experience, he couldn't remember it properly although he wanted to relive every detail, he couldn't recall how it had begun, exactly what had happened. Afterwards he hadn't been able to sleep and he had thought how different it had been to kissing Rose. He would never want to kiss a girl now. All day he had been impatient to see Reggie, yet increasingly terrified as the day went on in case Reggie made no indication that anything had occurred, would never mention it again. His thoughts had returned to Reggie each time he had been distracted by Gran. He found himself staring into space, forgetting time. When the back door opened at six o'clock and Reggie walked in his relief had been so intense he had felt weak. Gran had been sitting there and Dick introduced them and nothing might have happened between them they were so casual. It had been agonizing to listen to Gran talking, to answer politely. I've heard all this before, he wanted to shout at her. "I told Doctor I'd rather stay 'ere than go into any of those places. 'E said . . ."

Dick wondered what Reggie was thinking. If he was going to stay here again tonight he ought to tell Gran. He thought of him standing before the looking glass, wearing his trousers and sweater, combing his hair, as he had seen him this morning. It was strange how Reggie's appearance mattered to him. He had imagined him all day, he stared at him now. Before he could only have told you that Reggie had his hair cut short. Now he knew the colour of his eyes, the shape of his mouth, the thickness of his arms and legs, the width of his shoulders, the curve of his neck.

Ahead of them Les's car swerved to the side of the road and pulled up. They came up behind it and stopped too, and they all came on to the pavement, Reggie and Dick taking off their goggles and Les his unnecessary crash helmet. Les led the way into the house where he lived with his married sister in a top-floor flat. The house was similar to the one where Reggie and Dot had lived together, but Les had his own front door. Inside, in contrast to the threadbare linoleum on the stairs and the chipped paint surround, was a red-and-beige-patterned carpet in both the hall and Les's bed-sitting room and the walls were newly papered in red and gold stripes. In Les's room were a contemporary put-u-up, two chairs and a painted table. On the mantelpiece were two ornaments, one a pair of waxen legs emerging from a small net frill and the other a china Scottie dog with "Bonny Wee Fellow" written on the base. A calendar beside the fireplace had a picture of a voluptuous blonde in a tight red dress. Les went out of the room and came back with a half-bottle of whisky which he poured into tumblers. When they were drinking he put his feet up on his put-u-up, crossed his ankles and said, "This is 'ow we're going to do things on Friday."

" 'Ow many of us then?" asked Reggie. He had been surprised to find only the four of them at Nick's tonight.

"Us 'ere," said Les. "But we're doing it on be'alf of the 'ole gang. I reckon it don't do to 'ave a big crowd. Draws attention like."

They murmured agreement. Dick felt rather proud that he and Reggie had been chosen for this first venture.

"What I got plans for," Les went on, "is to 'ave little groups of us doing jobs all the time. And all sharing the lolly."

"If any of us gets nabbed it don't matter," said Shaved Head. "The others can still keep going."

"That's right," Les said. "Now about Friday. I been into it pretty thorough and you've all seen the lay-out. 'E goes to the bank Saturday and 'e don't live over the shop, I've followed 'im 'ome twice. And I've bought some fags just on closing time and he empties the till and puts it somewhere in the back."

"What about the law?" Reggie asked. "They walk about all night."

"I kept a look out the other night," Les said. "You don't think I 'adn't thought of it, do you?" He sounded aggressive. "No, 'e passes by three times, about quarter past one, quarter past three and a quarter past five. We want to be in there by two, and get out about 'alf past three."

"We going in that little side door, then?" said Dick. Les had taken them down the alleyway which ran alongside the shop.

"Of course, you stupid nut. You don't think we're going to smash the glass in the street, do you?" Les poured himself another whisky. "Okay?"

"Okay, Les."

"See you at Nick's Friday, then. But we don't leave together. We'll meet up in the alley."

As they rode home Reggie wondered if he ought to try to see Dot tomorrow. He felt responsible and although he had no intention of living with her again, he felt they should talk about their future. What about his future? Would he go on living with Dick's Gran? Sleeping in the same room as Dick? He had been shaken by last night. It had been so unintentional, so unforeseen and so compelling. He knew it wasn't just an instance, happening because of the particular circumstances. His feelings for Dick now were

68

like those he had had when he first met Dot. He was excited and anxious, on the point of loving. He thought, why should I feel like this over Dick, I'm not queer. But perhaps he was, if he felt as he did, although it had never happened before. He knew blokes often had sex together if there were no girls around, in the army and things. It didn't mean anything. But this did. It wasn't because there was nothing better. Perhaps last night it had been. He didn't know. But it wasn't now. Now it was deliberate and what he wanted.

As they began to climb the stairs to bed Gran called out, "I thought you'd 'ad a smash-up on that motor-bike."

Dick went into the room.

"We was just with friends, 'aving a drink. You mustn't worry about us, Gran." He kissed her, and as he went to the door he said, "Reggie come back with me again. You don't mind, do you?"

"I told you, you do what you like. You 'ave your pals 'ere when you feel like it."

His hand was on the door handle. He was aching to leave her.

"Could you just fill me 'ot-water bottle before you turn in? It's got cold."

He took it and went into the kitchen. He was on edge to go upstairs to Reggie. His hand trembled as he lit the gas burner. He sighed. He clenched and unclenched his hands. He walked about the room with impatience and irritation. He heard footsteps and looked round sharply as Reggie came into the kitchen and leant against the door. Their eyes met. They smiled. For a moment they couldn't look away. Then the kettle boiled and Dick filled the bottle and took it in to Gran and kissed her again and turned off the light. Reggie waited at the foot of the stairs and as Dick shut Gran's door he held out his hand to him and together they went upstairs.

"I don't like stealing," Reggie said. "Once you start you go on and it can't end up good."

Lying there in the dark Dick didn't want to talk about Friday. He turned on his side and put his arm across Reggie. There was so much in his mind that he hadn't the ability to express. He wanted to ask Reggie if he loved him, but it was embarrassing to talk about love, although he watched it in films and sang about it in songs. Songs suddenly seemed to have meaning for him. It wasn't

69

all tripe. He wanted to analyse his feelings and Reggie's, to talk about themselves and their relationship. But he didn't know the word "analyse" and he couldn't explain his longing. Nothing mattered in the world now. His life was quite bound up.

"Do you think about Dot, then?" he said at last.

"Yes," said Reggie. "I think about her a lot."

Dick hadn't expected this answer. He had intended it to be a leading question. He wanted Reggie to say "Not now I've met you." His words stopped being premeditated, and he asked, afraid, "Do you want to go back?"

"No," Reggie answered quickly. He paused. "I want to stay 'ere."

"I love you," Dick said. He couldn't believe he had said it and when Reggie didn't answer he wondered if in fact he had. He didn't know how to go on.

"When you kiss me and that," he said at last, nervously, "you don't pretend I'm a girl or anything?"

"Don't be daft," Reggie said. " 'Ow could I pretend you was a girl? You're the wrong shape."

That's not what I meant, thought Dick.

"I don't want to pretend you're a girl neither," Reggie said suddenly, his voice far louder than before.

"I don't think you are either," Dick said. "I mean I know you aren't but I wouldn't want you to be. I love you as you are." After a while he added, "It's funny, isn't it. I mean we don't want to put on lipstick or anything like that, do we?"

Dick woke to hear Gran's voice calling him from downstairs. It was still dark, and he tried to see Reggie's illuminated watch face on the bedside table, but it was upside down and he couldn't read it.

"Dickie, Dickie," came Gran's shout.

He leapt out of bed and ran downstairs. Her door was open and the light was on and he could see her standing just inside the room.

"What's up, Gran?" he asked. She was holding on to the side of her bed, leaning over.

"It's me 'ernia," she said. "It's ever such a bad pain tonight. You'd better get the doctor to push it back."

He remembered that Gran often had "attacks", when she couldn't eat and was in pain. He had heard his mother talk about it unkindly, saying Gran should have had an operation years

70

before, but that she was too scared to go into hospital. *He* was scared now. She was quite yellow and vomiting between words. The vomit was green.

"Come on, Gran," he said. "You get into bed." He took her arm and tried to heave her on to the bed, but she was too heavy and didn't seem able to help herself. He was terrified she was going to die. She was old and she seemed so ill.

"Reggie," he shouted. "Reggie, come down 'ere." He heard Reggie jump out of bed and run down the stairs. When he saw Gran he at once helped Dick to lift her on to the bed.

"I knew it was coming on this morning," Gran said. "I see gold wires in front of me eyes."

"You get the doctor," Dick said. "I'll stay with 'er."

Reggie climbed the stairs two at a time and pulled his trousers on over his pyjama trousers. He wasn't wearing a top, and hadn't time to put on anything but his leather cycling jacket.

"Where does 'e live?" he said, on his way to the front door.

"Thirty-seven Ringwood Road," Gran said. She clung to Dick's hand. "I can't push it back," she said. "It's getting bigger. It's as big as a pear." She seemed almost proud. "Oh, the pain's something chronic. I 'ope 'e'll be quick."

"'E's gone on the bike," Dick said. " 'As it 'appened before Gran?"

"Never as bad as this," she moaned. "I 'ad it when I was in labour, but it was never as bad as this."

"But that's fifty years ago," Dick said.

"I suffered a long time," Gran said. "Me truss don't do much good any more."

She looked enormous, stretched on the bed on her back. Her naked arms, lined with blue and black and green veins, were big and flabby. Millions of little creases covered the tops of her breast, and the breasts themselves seemed to lie under the nightdress like two jellyfish. Her broad bunioned feet pointed upward towards the ceiling.

Dick thought she was almost unconscious at times, then she groaned and held his hand tighter. He knew that if she wanted the doctor she must be feeling very ill.

"Do you think 'e'll make me go to the 'ospital?" she asked.

"Let's wait and see," Dick said. "Do you want anything, Gran? An 'ot-water bottle or a drink?"

"I don't want nothing," Gran said. "Nothing at all."

It was only fifteen minutes before Reggie arrived back on the

71

bike, and Dick heard the doctor's car draw up behind it and stop, and he ran to the door to let them in.

"I knew this would happen one day," the doctor said, pushing past Dick and going into the bedroom. "Come on, Granny, let me have a look."

Dick had followed him into the bedroom and stood there not wanting to watch but fascinated just the same. He saw the doctor lift up Gran's nightdress and look at the large lump at the bottom of her stomach, almost reaching the top of her leg.

"It's terrible, isn't it, Doctor," she said. "I can feel it's terrible. I can't get it back."

"I'll try," he said, and he put his hand on to the lump and pressed. "It won't go back, will it? I'm afraid we'll have to have it out."

"Oh no, Doctor, not out." Gran began to cry. "I'll never get out alive if they take me in there."

"You'll never leave here alive if you don't," he said brusquely. He opened his bag. "I'm going to give you an injection and then get an ambulance." He turned to Dick.

"This will take the pain away. I want you to pack her washing things. And you'd better get dressed yourself. You'll have to come down to the hospital and sign the form. She won't sign it herself."

Dick wished terribly that he wasn't alone in his responsibility. Gran seemed calmed almost at once by the injection.

"Keep an eye on 'er," he said to Reggie. "I'll get dressed." He felt he was in the middle of a dream, nothing had seemed real since he had been torn out of a deep sleep. Thank God Reggie had come back tonight. The doctor went out, slamming the door. Dick knew he could telephone the hospital from the box at the end of the road, so that it shouldn't be long before the ambulance came. He hurried downstairs again, combing his hair with his fingers. He couldn't find a case for Gran's things, only a big carrier bag from the grocer's. He put in her flannel and her false teeth, still swimming in the little pink box, and her big toothbrush with its flattened bristles.

"You'd better give 'er a towel," Reggie said, "and another nightdress. And 'er 'airbrush."

Dick found them and pushed them in, and put her handbag on top. If she died, he thought, what a shabby collection of possessions to leave behind.

He heard the ambulance draw up outside and went to the door

before the men rang the bell. Two men came in, carrying red blankets and pushing a wheelchair.

" 'Allo, Grandma," they said cheerfully. "Soon 'ave you better." They helped her up into the chair, and the pain seemed to have gone now for she smiled at the men and said bright, rather irrelevant things. They wrapped her up in the red blankets until only her face was visible.

"Father Christmas," said one man.

"I could go for you in that, you looking smashing," said the other almost at the same time.

Swiftly they wheeled Gran out of the house, her paper bag balanced on her lap. Dick and Reggie followed, not quite sure what to do.

"You go with 'er," Reggie said. "I'll follow on me bike and then I can fetch you 'ome."

Dick went into the ambulance with Gran. All his life he had wanted to see the inside of an ambulance but now he was so worried he forgot to look. He was only aware of the ambulance man and of Gran still sitting in the wheelchair, saying, "You're taking me a long way from 'ome," and the man replying, "Not as the crow flies," and Gran saying, "I'm not a crow, am I?"

At last they turned in at the hospital gates and Gran was swiftly wheeled down the slope and through the glass doors which swung back after her. Dick followed helplessly. At the reception desk he was asked to sign a form authorizing the operation. Gran seemed philosophical. "If I've got to 'ave it, I've got to, darling." The injection seemed to have changed her outlook.

The last Dick saw of her she was being wheeled into a large lift, and concealed behind clanging gates.

"Telephone in the morning," said the woman at the desk.

"Can't I phone sooner?" Dick asked.

"I don't think there will be anything to tell you before eight o'clock. We'll get in touch with you if there is anything important."

If she dies, thought Dick. He was sure she was going to die and that he had seen her for the last time. He went out into the hospital forecourt where Reggie was waiting beside his bike.

"I got to phone in the morning," Dick said.

"Lucky you was in the 'ouse," Reggie said. "If she'd been on 'er own she'd 'ave 'ad it, certain."

"I shouldn't think 'er chances are that 'ot now," said Dick. He felt choked and drained of energy. "Let's go 'ome."

"Get on, then," Reggie said. "We'll 'ave a cup of tea when we get there."

"I want more than tea," said Dick. Nothing mattered except Gran now, not even Reggie. He didn't want Gran to die. He didn't want her to die now.

NINE

"SHE's as well as can be expected," said the precise, deep female voice on the telephone. "She's had a successful operation."

"Can I see 'er?" asked Dick. This told him nothing except that she wasn't dead.

"Visiting is from six-thirty till seven."

"Thanks." Dick put down the receiver and pushed the door of the telephone booth open and went out into the street. Reggie had gone to work and he had nothing to do all day. He walked back home and made himself another pot of tea, wondering what he could take Gran, if it was silly to take flowers, if she was allowed to eat fruit. He realized suddenly that he had better tell his father and mother what had happened. He finished his tea, washed up his cup and left the tea-leaves for another pot when he came home. Then he tidied his hair and went out to the bus-stop to catch the bus to his parents' house. Gran had the front-door key in her bag, and feeling slightly guilty he left the back door unlocked.

His mother was cleaning the white step when he reached the gate.

"Not got a job, then?" she greeted him.

"Gran's ill," he said. "She's in 'ospital."

"Oh God," said his mother. "We don't seem to 'ave a week's peace."

He went into the house with her, and was aware how clean it smelt after Gran's house. The lino shone with polish, there wasn't dust anywhere.

"Well," his mother said, "what 'appened then?"

"It was 'er 'ernia. It strangulated or something."

"I'm not surprised," said his mother. "Did you see the thing she wore? A sort of truss the doctor give 'er in nineteen-ten. I told 'er for years, and your Dad did too, that something like this would 'appen. It's 'er own fault."

75

"I'm going up the 'ospital tonight," Dick said, " 'alf six."

"Well, there's no point in my fagging there too, is there? She won't feel like seeing more than one." She stared at him. "You coming 'ome now, I suppose?"

"No. I'm getting work there. I'll look after the 'ouse till she gets back."

"Don't kid yourself," said his mother unkindly, "she won't be going 'ome again. If she gets over the operation she'll 'ave to be looked after properly. There's no arguing this time."

"Well, I'm nearer the 'ospital there," Dick said. They couldn't make him go home. He was eighteen. "And I'm getting work."

"Do what you like," his mother said surprisingly. "You're not 'appy at 'ome with us so you might as well stay there."

Dick thought, She likes me to be away. At least I'm quite free now. But his freedom was all at once perilous because if Gran was too frail to live at home what would happen to him and Reggie? "I might get a room with a mate," he said, "if I can't stay at Gran's."

"Well, unemployment benefit wouldn't go far," his mother said. "You don't know 'ow much living costs."

"I'll manage," said Dick.

Dick stood with six other people outside the swing doors of the Annie Pilchurch ward. Through the tiny squares of glass he could see nurses' caps bobbing and floral screens being folded away from round the beds. He held a bunch of sweet-peas, picked from his mother's carefully cultivated garden.

A nurse suddenly appeared at the door and said, "You may come in now," and the other people hurried in and dispersed to various beds and Dick stood on the threshold looking for Gran. He saw her at last, at the far end of the ward, and he hurried down the polished gangway, past the sister seated at a desk in the centre, to where Gran lay, not looking towards the door. She was even yellower than last night, and a thin tube emerged from her nose, secured to her cheek by a piece of sticking plaster. There was an enormous bruise on her arm and another on her hand.

" 'Allo, Gran," he said.

She moved her head slightly. "'Allo, darling. I didn't think you'd come."

"Of course I'd come." He threw the sweat-peas onto the bed-spread. "Mum sent these."

"They know, then?"

76

"I went down this morning. 'Ow do you feel."

"Awful," said Gran. "I got another of these tubes coming out of me stomach. The doctor 'ere says I was lucky they was able to act so quick. Me leg was going rotten, mouldering."

"Gangrene," said the woman in the next bed, leaning forward. "It's called gangrene. This your grandson?"

"That's right," said Gran.

"Wonderful, isn't she?" said the woman to Dick.

"Ain't it pretty 'ere," said Gran, "the curtains and things. I think it's lovely."

"It's all right," said Dick.

"I come round fighting. Look at me bruises. That's where the needle went in," she said, pointing to the one on her arm. "Count, 'e said to me, and that's all I remember. Isn't it wonderful?"

Dick nodded.

"I won't never 'ave to wear me truss again. They said it was doing me no good. Wonderful, isn't it?"

"What did you go on wearing it for then?"

"How was I to know? Doctor never said nothing. I 'ad it forty-nine years. It cost a lot when I 'ad it."

One of the nurses, young and pretty and Irish, came over and picked up the sweet-peas. "Aren't they beautiful? I'll put them in some water for you."

"Thank you, love," Gran said to Dick. "We got some lovely nurses, ever so gentle they are. Black ones too."

The sister rang a handbell.

"That's time," said the woman in the next bed. "My turn tomorrow. My sister comes up from Staines on a Wednesday."

Dick bent and kissed Gran. He thought she looked dreadful, ten years older and terribly ill.

"'By, Gran, see you tomorrow."

"It's afternoon tomorrow," said the woman in the next bed.

"Thanks." He walked swiftly out of the ward, ran down the four flights of stone steps and through the forecourt to the bus-stop. Reggie was at home and they were going to the pictures. They weren't going to Nick's tonight. Les would wonder where they had got to, but they wanted to be alone.

Neither Dick nor Reggie had done anything like shop-breaking before. Dick was less moral than Reggie and had the opportunity occurred he would probably have taken part. Now he was quite pleased at the chance of getting easy money and particularly glad because it meant he could really help Gran without working. Although he had talked about getting a job he didn't really want to. Reggie, however, would have preferred to lead a conventional life. If he had married a different girl, and had had children and an organized home he would have been really happy. But because Dot had forced him to go out and Nick's had provided the boys and subsequently Dick, he accepted the situation. Besides, he wanted to be with Dick and years of seeing second-rate films and reading poorly written paperback novels made him believe in the romantic comradeship between two men engaged in law-breaking. Standing beside Dick in the alleyway at half past two on Saturday morning he felt protective and affectionate. He thought if Dick was copped he would give himself up too.

"Easy as 'aving a piss," said Shaved Head, as the lock broke with a small clicking noise. "'E was asking to be broke into." He opened the narrow back door into the shop and they all hurried inside. He closed the door and the panel over it, filled with amber-coloured glass, gave a dim light. Les shone his black rubber torch. A stained sink with one tap was fixed to the wall beside the door. A naked bulb hung on a long flex that had been looped and knotted. In front of them, directly facing the back door, was a door into the room behind the shop. Les opened it and they followed him in. It was a combination of stock-room and sitting-room. Two walls were covered with shelves and a big cupboard. The wall with the window in it had a table, a chair and a wireless-set on the sill. There was also another small table with a drawer and a pile of paid newspaper bills pierced with a spike.

"Now," Les said. "Let's see what we can find."

They began to sweep things off the shelves, not quite sure what to do.

"'Ave some fags," Les suggested. Dick pocketed a lighter. Les opened the cupboard door. "Not even a f...... key," he said. Inside, in two black metal deed-boxes, were, they assumed, the takings.

"Come on, Reggie, you got the tools. Open them, then."

Reggie took them and sat down at the table. He took a screw-driver out of his pocket and inserted it into one of the locks, twisted it and levered it off.

"Too easy, ain't it," said Les. Reggie opened the lid, it was full of silver screwed in perforated bank bags.

"The other's got the notes," Reggie said, "it ain't so 'eavy."

He broke that lock too, the others looking over his shoulder.

"Count it," said Les excitedly.

"Not 'ere," said Reggie. "Let's go while we got the chance."

"What about the rozzer?"

"What's the time?"

"Three."

"We'd better 'ang on till 'e's gone. Count it."

They grouped round the table and silently counted the money, flattening the notes, piling the coins, the only sounds their breathing, the rustle of paper and the clink of metal.

"Thirty-five quid 'ere," said Reggie.

"Fifteen," said Dick.

"'Undred and thirty," said Les, almost shouting. "One bleeding 'undred and thirty nicker, mate."

"Let's flog the lighters too," said Dick.

"What's the time?"

"We can go now. 'E must 'ave gone."

"We're meeting the cats at my place for the share-out. I'll go first." Les went to the back door and hurried to the end of the alleyway and looked up and down the street.

"Okay, boys."

They followed him out, walking silently.

"I'll go first," Les said again. "You wait 'ere while I fetches the car. When I pull up throw the boxes in the back, then f......off." He left the alley and began to walk briskly along the pavement, leaving Dick and Reggie with the deed-boxes. Dick put out his hand and pressed Reggie's arm.

"It's not bad, is it?"

"By the time they've all 'ad a pick there won't be much for us," said Reggie. He felt that having gone against his conscience there should be more reward.

In a few minutes they saw Les's car come slowly and quietly down the street. Shaved Head was in the back and opened the rear door as the car drew up. Reggie and Dick bundled the boxes in and the car drew away.

"Come on," Dick said. "We can go now." They ran along the road in the opposite direction to the one Les had taken, and reached the bike. Dick felt almost disappointed. It had been too easy, too uneventful. He had expected to get a kick out of it and he hadn't.

"I think I'll give the money to Dot," Reggie said, putting his leg over the saddle.

"Give it to Dot," Dick echoed. "What for? You don't owe it 'er."

"I do in a way," Reggie said.

Dick was resentful. "You've left 'er, ain't you?"

"I got to talk to 'er some time. I'll take the money with me."

"But you're not going back to 'er, are you?"

"No. I told you."

"Seeing 'er you might change your mind?"

"Oh, shut it," Reggie said. "You keep on about it. I told you, I'm staying with you."

Les and Shaved Head and the other boys were waiting at the flat when Dick and Reggie arrived. Les was sitting on the floor, the others standing around.

Les poured himself a whisky from the bottle beside him. "'Ow many of us? Ten. I'll do the counting." He began to divide the money into equal parts. As he handed each of them a share he said, "I got another on for next week, a little Jew tailor's place. I bet 'e thinks 'e got everything locked away safe. And the week after I was thinking about the Ritz cinema. We ought to make an 'undred each, easy, with both those."

Dick and Reggie put their money into the inside zipped pockets of their jackets.

"Be seeing you."

"'Night."

They closed the door behind them and ran down to the street.

Dick went through the hospital doors without yesterday's timidity. Not only did he know his way up to the ward, but he felt good. He was cocksure. He had twenty pounds in his pocket, which wasn't a great deal, not much more than a week's wages, but he hadn't earned it, he had taken it. And this gave him a thrill. He had outwitted the shop-owner and the police, he had broken the law and not been caught. He could give Gran fifteen quid, and she would be grateful and touched and happy. And he had Reggie.

The people outside the ward doors were, with one exception, the same people he had seen there yesterday. He smiled at them and said "Hallo", and they smiled back. He felt warm towards them, they were in sympathy with one another, there for the same purpose, equally worried, equally bored by the daily visit, equally ready to make it. The same nurse opened the doors to let them in. The familiarity put him at ease and he walked down the ward as if he had been coming there for years.

Gran looked better. The tube was out of her nose, and her hair had been brushed by one of the nurses and plaited neatly. She had been allowed to eat a little today, she said, as he approached the bed. And it was lovely food. Dick was relieved to see that the sister from Staines had arrived and was busily talking to the woman in the next bed. At least she wouldn't notice that he was giving Gran money. He didn't want other people to know. They might ask her to lend it, or even pinch it out of her locker. You couldn't trust people.

Dick sat on the canvas-and-metal chair by her bed.

"What does the doctor say?" he asked. "Is 'e pleased with you?"

"'E thinks I'm marvellous for me age," Gran said happily. "They all do. The nurses all want to do me 'air."

Dick couldn't think why they should. Still, they had to make interest for themselves, nursing old women all day.

"What's 'appening at 'ome?" Gran asked. "'Oo's looking after the 'ouse?"

"I am," said Dick, who hadn't done a thing since she left except to wash the cups and plates he and Reggie were actually using. He hadn't even made the bed yesterday, but Reggie was fed up when he came home and wouldn't get in it until they had straightened it. "The 'ome 'elp comes, doesn't she?"

"Tuesdays," said Gran.

"I must 'ave been out when she came, then," Dick said. "Will they stop 'er now you're in 'ere?"

"I don't know," Gran said. "The almoner's coming up to 'ave a chat with me. She's a lovely lady, Mrs. Ellerman says." She looked at the lady in the next bed as she spoke.

Dick put his hand in his pocket. "I got some money for you, Gran."

"Money? Where did you get money from?"

"We went up to the dogs." He pulled out fifteen pound notes. "Fifteen nicker."

Gran looked at it incredulously. "You was lucky, wasn't you? Didn't know you 'ad that much to lose."

"I went with a dollar," Dick said. "It was my lucky night."

"When I was first married it would 'ave taken Dad three weeks to bring 'ome that lot."

"That wasn't much, was it?" Dick put the money down beside the sponge-bag on her locker shelf. Why shouldn't we go

81

to the dogs? he was thinking. I might get back what I've given Gran. And if I lose it doesn't matter. There's this job of Les's next week.

"I can't take it," Gran protested. "You spend it on yourself. And what about your Mum? She could do with it."

"I want you to 'ave it," Dick said.

"Well, I can't keep it 'ere. And I can't 'ave it put in me post-office book. They come to look at it and if they see I got any extra they'll cut the assistance."

"Keep it under your mattress," Dick said, "or in your corsets. I'll try and win you some more."

The nurse rang the bell. "Time's up, everyone."

"Shall I come tomorrow?" he asked Gran.

"If you got the time. I like to see you. I might write some letters if you bring me some paper and envelopes."

"I'll get the stamps too."

"They sell stamps 'ere, Dick," she called him back. "Take the money and keep it for me at 'ome. I can't 'ave it in me locker. They'll see it."

"All right," he said, going back and putting it back in his pocket. "But it's yours for when you come 'ome. I'm not touching it."

"Use it if you need it," Gran called after him as he walked out of the ward.

TEN

DICK had never felt so happy as he did now. His affair with Reggie, the stolen money and the fun of stealing gave his life a new dimension. This was living, he told himself. He wanted it to go on for ever. He was confident, exuberant. When he reported at the labour exchange, as he had to each week, he talked with a new insolence. He had spent the fifteen pounds he had brought home from Gran on a pair of leather jeans which he had wanted for weeks. It didn't matter. Gran wasn't there to know and he would be able to replace it as soon as the next job was completed.

He went by bus to the shop in Clapham which specialized in motor-cycling kit and made-to-measure. He made particular specifications. He wanted big white stitching and an extra pocket. When, five days later, the flat parcel arrived, he couldn't wait to put them on. He ran up to the bedroom, cut the coarse string with a razor blade and tore off the paper. He changed into them and stood on the bed so that he could see his legs in the mirror. Then he got his jacket and tried it on with them. He thought he looked wonderful. He longed to show himself to Reggie. He combed his hair. He was growing narrow sideboards and carefully shaved round the dark beginnings every day. Gently he combed the stubble. He took off his jacket, put on a white tee shirt and the jacket again. He decided to go down to the garage and show Reggie. He loved the slight stiffness of his jeans as he walked. He thought he ought to buy a bike. Why not? He knew how to get the money. And he had his licence. He had often borrowed Dad's machine.

Reggie was having his morning tea-break. He was sitting on the step of the small office, his white overalls undone at the neck, exposing the cross on a silver chain which he always wore. He grinned when he saw Dick.

"You need a machine now, mate."

"Just what I was thinking."

"You know you was saying about the dogs? Well, 'ow about going up to 'Arringay tonight? I could do with a bit extra."

Dick had lost his enthusiasm for the idea. He couldn't understand Reggie's reluctance to do another job. He sat down close beside him on the step.

"We don't need to go there for extra, do we?"

"I'd rather do it that way. I got to give Dot something. I spent the twenty nicker from the other night, you know I 'ave. I do owe it 'er, really. I got to go and see 'er."

Dick wanted to take Reggie's hand, but he couldn't because there were other people around.

"Can't we go away for a bit?" Away from Dot.

"Where to? Anyway, you ain't got a job like I 'ave. I can't go away."

"I didn't mean an 'oliday. I was thinking we might get a ship." The idea had come to him as he was speaking. He wouldn't be able to live at Gran's much longer. Reggie might get tired of sharing rooms with him. But if they went to sea they would be together, away from the disruptions of home. He had never wanted to go abroad before. Uncle Arthur had taken coach holidays in recent years, to Holland and Switzerland. Now Dick remembered the postcard views he had brought back with him and he imagined himself and Reggie in such places.

"I dunno," Reggie said. He stood up. "I got to do some work now. See you tonight."

"Okay." Dick stood up too. "Think it over, mate."

Reggie nodded. "We going up the dogs, then?"

"If you like." Dick watched him go over to the car on which he was working and wriggle under the chassis until only his legs in the oil-stained overalls showed. Then he turned and walked slowly home. On the way he looked into Nick's, but it was quite different in the daytime. Several workmen sat at the tables, drinking cups of tea and eating small meat pies and sandwiches. It was difficult to believe it was so exciting at night.

He shopped on the way home for his and Reggie's supper. They had fish-and-chips most nights, or sausages. Today he bought ham and a loaf of bread. He carried the bread under his arm. As he walked along the street he kept thinking about the Merchant Navy. It was a smashing idea. He wondered how you signed on. He'd find out all about it and then tell Reggie. He'd ask at the labour exchange. No, he wouldn't do that, better not show his face there too often – he would go down to Southampton

84

in the morning, by train, and ask at the docks. Reggie would be at work and wouldn't know he'd gone. He didn't want Reggie to know. He might think Dick was acting for him, being too sure and possessive. It was better to go on the quiet. He began to day-dream about himself and Reggie on board ship. They'd probably have to scrub decks, and they would sleep in hammocks. Did sailors really sleep in hammocks? Or was that just in films? And they would go ashore in exotic places and sometimes be at sea for weeks on end. He thought he would feel really safe if he and Reggie were together at sea. No one could take Reggie away from him then.

It was raining. They parked the bike in a little street near the arena. Even with a small cycle it was difficult to find a place. It was eight o'clock and they had missed the first race.

"It don't matter," Reggie said. "One race won't make all that difference." Dick hadn't been to the dogs before, although he didn't tell Reggie. He was ashamed of his ignorance. He had five pounds in his pocket. Reggie had ten. Reggie had bought new lights for his bike out of his share of the money. He was sorry now that he hadn't given it to Dot straight away and finished with her. He felt that by giving Dot some money he would be doing the right thing. He believed he would no longer feel guilty, as he did, in spite of everything, if he helped her financially. Then she could use the money to get rid of the baby if she wanted. They had lent money in the past to Dot's unmarried, pregnant friends. Or else she could keep it, both the money and the baby. It would buy some clothes or something. He wanted to talk to Dot, too, about getting divorced. For Dick's sake he wanted to be quite free. Dick was so scared he was going to go back to her. He was crazy. Reggie was much happier now that he had left her. He wasn't worried, there seemed no complications. He and Dick enjoyed going out together, and if they did join the Merchant Navy, as Dick suggested, it would take them away from Nick's and the gang. Reggie didn't want to go on leading this sort of life. He'd end up inside if he did.

They turned into the entrance of the arena. Rows of parked taxis waited in the car-park to take the winners home. They walked along the pavement, bounded by a high concrete wall, to the ticket barriers. Out of the row of small green doors, rather like those in a public lavatory, tailed long queues of men. Reggie and Dick joined the one directly in front of them. Inside they could hear music being relayed noisily through the loudspeakers. They edged slowly until it was their turn to pay three shillings each for programmes, and then they clicked through the turnstile into the arena.

It was enormous, far bigger than Dick had anticipated. The track itself was a large uncluttered oval. There were stalls selling jellied eels and winkles and white-coated men carrying trays of hot dogs and sweets and peanuts. The bookies stood on little boxes shouting the odds and white-gloved tick-tac men at their sides semaphored to one another. At the opposite side of the track was the big glass-fronted restaurant and the expensive seats. At the far end of the oval was the tote and nearest to it the covered stands. They pushed through the crowds on to the long shallow steps under a protective roofing. The rain, lit by the big track lights, looked like millions of slanting threads of white cotton. Dick looked at the people round him. They were almost all men, and they appeared to him to be mostly poor men, the sort of man his grandfather had been, cloth caps and white scarves. Their faces were lined, and, he felt, grimed. There were some odd-looking men too, the kind one found at all-night cafés and in some pubs, with pale, curiously-featured faces, and the collars of their coats turned up. One or two prim-looking women with plastic rain-hoods stood with their husbands. They looked out of place amongst so many men. On the little slates the odds changed.

"Well," Reggie said, looking at his programme. "I fancy Romany in the next race. Look at 'is time, three lengths better than any of them. I'm going to put five quid on. The odds is five to two."

"I will too, then," said Dick. It was all he had, but he didn't understand, and if Reggie thought it was the best thing to do he would take his word for it. He pulled the money out of his wallet and handed it to Reggie. He watched Reggie go over to the nearest bookie and pay and receive a small card in exchange. Reggie took a piece of pencil out of his pocket and did sums on the programme.

"Thirty-five nicker if we win," he said.

There was a fanfare of trumpets over the loudspeakers and six men began to lead the dogs round the track. Behind them followed another, carrying a brush and dustpan.

"That's ours," said Reggie excitedly, "the dog in the orange coat." The dog's waterproof shone with rain. "'Ee ought to run well, even in the wet."

The procession approached the traps which were being dragged into position. Dick thought they looked like rabbit hutches.

"Come on," urged Reggie, "let's go down to the rails."

Dick followed him into the rain. The dogs were howling in the traps, one was still being persuaded in, and the two men gave him a push and shut the door. A bell rang. The arena lights dimmed, leaving the track brilliantly lit. The mechanical hare suddenly appeared, bobbing down the track. As it passed the traps the dogs were released and went hurtling after it.

"Look at 'im," yelled Reggie. "'E's got the rails. 'E's going to do it." The dog was a good length ahead. Dick couldn't believe their luck. The dogs tore past the finishing post, the orange-coated one still in the lead.

"This is the way to do it," Reggie shouted happily. He joined the queue to collect his winnings. Dick stayed leaning against the rails. The rain soaked his hair and trickled down his forehead into his eyes. He was so happy the discomfort didn't matter. Oddly it contributed to his happiness. His parents were mad, counting and saving, when money was as easy as this. Reggie came and stood beside him dividing the notes.

"There you are, mate. 'Ow's that?"

"Smashing," said Dick.

Reggie studied the programme intently. "I reckon Kingfisher Rose'll win this one. We'll put a score on."

"Each?" asked Dick. It seemed a lot to risk.

"Each," said Reggie.

Dick gave him the money and while Reggie went to place the bets Dick went over to a stall. Plates of cockles, whelks, mussels and jellied eels were arranged on a marble slab. He bought two saucers of jellied eels, and when Reggie left the bookie he shouted to him to come over. He thought the whole place was like a fairground, with the music and the stalls and the excitement and the open air.

They finished their eels and walked back through the crowds to where they had been standing before. They were taller than most of the people there and were conspicuous in their black clothes. A policeman, recognizable by his sports jacket, blue shirt and uniform trousers, eyed them warily. The fanfare blared again and the parade of dogs began. Dick and Reggie went to the rails again.

"That's ours," Reggie said, "the one in black."

The race started. The hare rushed by and the dogs, noses down, ran after it. In a few seconds the dog in the black coat was in front.

"Christ!" gasped Reggie. "We're going to do it again."

The dog won easily and Reggie collected the money. He couldn't believe his good fortune. And it was honest money. He wasn't risking his neck every time he breathed. He decided to embark on a more complicated form of betting which he tried to explain to Dick.

"Don't tell me," Dick said. "I'll just collect after."

"Well, we'll do a forecast combination, three dogs at ten nicker a time."

"Sounds all right," said Dick, handing over the money.

The race was about to begin. It was nine o'clock.

"I can't believe it," Dick said. "We won about an 'undred and eighty, ain't we, Reggie?"

"It'll be more with this," Reggie said. "You watch our dogs, Dick. One, five and six. Those are the ones you got to watch."

The hare passed the traps and the dogs were released. It was so familiar to Dick now that he felt he had been coming for years. One, five and six broke evenly and led to the first bend.

"We're in again," said Reggie, laughing. "We'll scoop the pool on this one."

On the back straight number four started to make ground rapidly, taking the lead at the fourth bend.

"Come on, Four!" shrieked the crowd. A woman beside Dick, elderly, flushed, her glasses in her hand, screamed with excitement. "Four, Four, Four!"

"Six," shouted Dick. "Go on, Six."

"It's no good, mate," said Reggie. "Save your breath. We've 'ad it." The race was over.

"Let's go," Dick said. "We've still got a few quid."

"I dunno," Reggie answered, staring at his programme. "I reckon we can get it back on the nine-thirty. This one 'ere," he pointed to the list of runners. "'E made better time than the first dog we won on. This track, mate. 'E's a cert, I should say."

"I don't want to lose what we 'ave got left," Dick persisted.

The woman beside them had been listening. "Number three in this race. I'm putting ten quid on 'im. 'E's certain to do it."

"That's the one," Reggie agreed excitedly. "That's the one I said, Dick. Number Three."

"'E's a good dog," said the woman. "I always pick up me losses on 'im if 'e's running."

"What do you say? Shall we put the lot on? We could make it all up and more if 'e wins?" Reggie faced Dick.

Dick pulled out the notes he had left and handed them to Reggie. "Okay, mate. Whatever you say."

It was the last race of the evening. The dogs began to run. Before they started Dick had the feeling their dog would lose. He wasn't a gambler. He had no optimism. They had lost once and they probably would lose again. The dogs streaked past them, number three one from last.

"We've 'ad the lot this time," he said to Reggie. With a pin-sharp shock of realization Reggie knew that the money they had won and the money they had brought with them was gone.

"Thanks for the tip," he said bitterly to the woman.

"I've never seen 'im run so badly. 'E was doped. That's what 'e was. Doped."

Reggie shrugged and turned away. Neither of them spoke as they left the arena, past the queues waiting for winnings, out with the crowds into the wet roadway where the puddles splashed their feet and legs. Opposite was a row of coffee bars and cafés.

"Want anything?" Dick asked.

Reggie shook his head. It was all too chancy, he thought. Dick was right. The Merchant Navy was the best thing for them. But he would see Dot first. He was never going to the dogs again. All the risk in raiding the shop had been for nothing and now he supposed they would have to do something else so that Dick could give his Gran some money and he could see Dot was all right. When they climbed on to the bike and Dick put his arms round him he felt, for the first time, a burst of irritation. He kicked the starter fiercely and drove fast, away from North London, across the river and home. Outside Gran's house he said, "I'll see you later. I'm going round to Dot's."

Dick seemed to go cold. "What for? You 'aven't got no money. She'll be asleep."

"I'll wake 'er, then. I want to 'ave a talk to 'er."

Dick got off the bike and stood on the pavement.

"I want to tell 'er I'll get 'er some money. So she knows I 'aven't forgotten."

"'Ow you going to get money, then?" Dick asked. "I thought you wasn't going with Les again."

"Not the dogs," Reggie shouted as he drove away.

ELEVEN

REGGIE still had the door-key to the house. He left the bike a street away, afraid that if he came too near he would disturb the landlady and warn Dot. Inexplicably he wanted to take Dot by surprise. He opened the front door and held the latch with his finger to stop any noise, letting it spring into position only when the door was closed. Then he went upstairs. The light in the room was on. He could see it through the half-inch outline of the door. He wondered if Dot would be alone. He was nervous and his breathing was shallow. He would have liked to turn and go downstairs again, and it was with a conscious effort of will that he turned the handle and went in.

Dot was sitting up in bed reading a comic. There was a crumpled chocolate wrapper on the eiderdown. She looked up startled and their eyes met.

"Well!" She stared at him. "You've got a cheek."

"I wanted to talk to you," Reggie said.

"You didn't 'ave to pick this time."

"I was passing."

They were silent and Reggie walked over to one of the armchairs and sat down. The room and Dot were both so familiar and yet he felt detached. He knew every detail and he couldn't feel he had lived there.

"Well, say what you come for and let's get some sleep." Dot pushed her comic away.

"I'm not coming back."

"I wouldn't 'ave you back."

Reggie looked at the floor and then at his hands. "Are you 'aving this baby then?"

"Yeah." She was three days late. It was likely.

"What are you going to do about it?"

"There's not much I can do, is there? I 'aven't the money to get rid of it."

91

"Would you if you 'ad?" he asked eagerly.

"I might."

"I'll get you some," he said. "I'll give it you before I go."

"Go?"

"I'm joining the Merchant Navy."

"Where's the money coming from?"

"Never you mind. I'll get it. And I'll get you plenty."

Dot looked at him curiously.

"You never 'ad no money. If you did it would go on that bike."

Reggie stood up. "I'll give it you next week. That won't be too late, will it? You can still 'ave it done then?"

"Yeah," said Dot. "I can still 'ave it done."

When Reggie had gone she lay awake thinking about him. She didn't need the money, if she wanted an abortion she could have it on credit, two pounds down and two a week until the thirty asked for by the woman in Earl Street was paid off. Reggie was up to something dodgy. She would find out what it was.

Dick was in bed but not asleep when Reggie came home. He heard the bike and although he had been sitting up with the light on, he quickly switched it off and lay down, pretending to be dozing. He didn't want Reggie to know he had been anxious. In fact he had been tense with worry, quite unable to lie down and relax. He had got out of bed several times and gone into the bathroom and looked out of the window to see if he could see Reggie. Each time he had heard the distant engine of a motor-cycle, and sometimes even a car, his heart had thumped and then he had felt disappointed and miserable when the noise had died away. Now, as Reggie's footsteps sounded on the stairs, he realized how silly he had been in thinking that Reggie had left him and gone back to Dot. When the door opened and he saw Reggie silhouetted there he couldn't feign sleep any longer and he swallowed and said, "Hallo," and Reggie said, "Hi," and came in and sat on the edge of the bed, still in his outdoor clothes.

"I told Dot I'd get 'er some money," he said.

Dick didn't answer and Reggie suddenly brushed his hand across his forehead and said, "It's the last time. I'm not doing nothing after this time. We'll get a ship, like you said."

Dick took his hand out of the bedclothes and held Reggie's. He was so happy he couldn't speak.

"We'll do this one on our own," Reggie said. "There ain't enough in it, with the others."

"Last night."

"Did 'e?" Les nodded. "'Ear that, boys? Reggie's promising money."

Dot suddenly began to be afraid.

"'E 'asn't said nothing to us, 'as 'e, boys?"

"No." "No, Les." "'E ain't said nothing to us."

"And 'ow much money did 'e kindly promise, may I ask?"

"I don't see what it's got to do with you," Dot said.

Les took her arm and held it at an uncomfortable angle.

"It's got everything to do with us. Reggie don't do things on 'is own." He twisted Dot's arm a fraction. "'Ow much?"

"'E didn't say, honest. 'E just said plenty."

"Reggie ain't got plenty, 'as 'e, boys?"

"'E bought them lights for 'is bike."

"And what else did Reggie say to you, darling?"

"Let go of me." Dot tried to get free.

"Not till you've opened that little mouth of yours a good bit wider. Where's 'e going to get this money?"

"'E didn't say. 'E didn't tell me nothing."

"Nothing?" Les twisted her arm again.

"Let 'er go, Les," said Carol.

"You shut it, or you'll get it after."

"'E said 'e was going in the Merchant Navy," Dot shouted. "And I don't blame 'im, wanting to get away from you lot."

Les dropped her arm.

"'Ear that, boys? 'E's going in the Merchant Navy. Not 'ere tonight, is 'e?"

"No," Shaved Head said, "nor 'is mate."

"I shouldn't be surprised they was thinking of pulling off a little job together," Les said. "I think we'd better keep them company for a little while. Not so they'd notice, of course."

Dot began to cry. "You're not to 'urt 'im."

"'Urt 'im?" Les appealed to the others. "'Ave I ever 'urt anybody?"

"I wish I 'adn't come," Dot said.

"We're very glad you did, darling. We'll look after Reggie for you. I don't suppose 'e'll feel like joining the Merchant Navy after a little chat with us."

"I'm going," Dot said. She pushed past Les, who didn't move to let her by. She ran out into the street, still crying. I know they're going to hurt him, she thought. She wondered if she should go to the police. But what could she tell them? She didn't know

95

what Reggie was going to do, or what Les was going to do to Reggie. It was all in her imagination. She was desperately frightened by what she had done. Her own motive seemed lost and mean now. She had meant to get her own back on Reggie, to have been able to threaten him perhaps. But it had become out of hand and dangerous. She didn't dare tell Reggie. He would never forgive her. There was nothing she could do. She was terrified and helpless. She wasn't even pregnant. Her period had started this morning. She could only go home and wait. She was guilty and alone.

Dick stepped on to the platform at Southampton. Reggie knew he was going now, and was pleased and anxious and even excited by it. Last night they had talked for hours, and Reggie had said they must join the Merchant Navy as soon as possible, get a ship directly the job at the cinema was done. As they had lain in bed, they kissed and talked about it, planned and re-planned. It seemed suddenly as if all their problems were on the point of being resolved, and they would be responsible only to themselves, that Gran and Dot and Les would no longer be on their consciences. And they would be earning money, be together, and see the world. Once they had the money from the cinema they felt they could discharge themselves from the past without the guilt they now suffered. Dot and Gran would be paid off, so to speak. Their parents didn't care and didn't matter. Reggie had said it was his chance to make a new life, forget his mistakes. He wanted to go straight, he said, and live honestly. Dick had answered that it was what he wanted too, although he didn't mean it. He only wanted Reggie, whatever keeping him entailed. He would steal, lie or kill to keep Reggie. He was burdened by his love for Reggie, full of jealousy and anxiety. All he wanted was for this episode to be over, and to be with Reggie, far away, at sea.

He could smell the sea from where he was standing, and see the funnels of ships. He had thought it was going to be a station like any other, but it was different and made him feel he was on the edge of a new life.

As he gave up his ticket at the barrier he asked the man where he should go to find out about joining the Merchant Navy. The ticket collector called over a porter and repeated the question.

"Shipping Federation Office," said the porter, and with much pointing and gesticulating directed him.

Dick walked through the town first. The shops were modern

96

and the window displays attractive. Better than at home, he thought. He liked new buildings, not because of the architecture but because he thought it was up to date. He had no time for the past. Anything before his own middle-teens was "old-fashioned".

He found the Shipping Federation Office near the docks. There were queues of men and he was reminded of the queues at the dogs. These men were mostly young and rough-looking, though a few wore the sort of suit he did when he was going out for an evening. Every twentieth man was in his late thirties and had the kind of weather-beaten face he associated with old sailors. He joined the queue nearest to him and moved very slowly forward until he was in the office.

"Yes?" said the man behind the desk.

"I want to ask about getting a ship next week. Me and another bloke. We don't care where it's going."

"Over there," said the man. "Next."

Dick joined the end of another line of men and waited again. When at last he came to the top he repeated his question.

"I want to ask about getting a ship next week. I'm asking for me and my mate."

"What have you been doing?" asked the uniformed man.

"Labouring," Dick answered. "I'm a builder's labourer."

"Been to sea before?"

"No, but I've always wanted to." He felt this was the right reply to make.

"Have you brought your references?"

Dick didn't know he needed references. He couldn't imagine which of his many past employers would write well of him in any case.

"I forgot 'em," he told the man. He thought perhaps Gran would write one out for him, and Reggie wrote nicely too. They could sign Doctor or The Reverend, or whatever was needed.

"Well, bring them with you next time. You'll have to join the union, and then have a medical. Then we'll see what ship is sailing. There will be an immigrant ship sailing in about twelve days. The *Armada*. You might get that as a steward."

"Thanks," said Dick. "I'll do all that then." He added as an afterthought, "Where's she sailing?"

"Australia."

Dick wormed his way past the queues and out into the street. Australia. That was the other side of the world. You dug a hole deep enough and you came out in Australia. He didn't know any-

97

thing about it except that it had sheep farms. He had learned about sheep farms at school. The fields didn't have hedges to divide them. A field was miles wide.

He went down to the docks to look at the ships. At the gates he was stopped for a pass. He didn't know he had to have a pass.

"Where do I get one?" he asked. The man at the gates sent him to an office.

"What do you want a pass for, son?"

"I got a mate on one of the ships," he said. "I want to see 'im."

"Okay." It was so easy. He retraced his steps and this time went through the dockyard gates. The *Queen Elizabeth* was in. He recognized her from the two red-and-black funnels. There were other big liners too. He read the names painted on their sides. Cargo was being loaded, derricks and cranes and crates divided and blocked the landscape. Men were working, stripped to the waist, others hurried about between the buildings and sheds. Next week it will be me, he thought. Reggie and me going up a gangplank, living on a ship, right out at sea, right away from land. He had never been on a ship in his life. He could scarcely imagine being cut off from England, being away from South London even. He was hot and thirsty and turned back towards the town to get a drink.

He walked back up the main street, passing the ancient Norman gateway straddling the new thoroughfare. He turned in a doorway of a modern pub, built at the end of a line of post-war shops. He went across to the bar and ordered a pint. There were several young men in the saloon bar and he was sure they were Merchant Seamen. He took his drink and sat down near a group of them and listened to their conversation. They were talking about another sailor who had been stopped by the customs and charged heavily on a present he had brought home for his girl-friend.

One of the group went off to fill their glasses. Dick turned to the boy next to him.

"Excuse me, mate. You're in the Merchant Navy, ain't you?" The boy looked at him. "Yeah, that's right."

"I'm 'oping to join next week."

"What line you joining then?"

"I don't know," said Dick sheepishly. He should have asked. "The ship's called the *Armada*."

"Oh, she's on loan to the government, trooping and that sort of thing."

"Yes," said Dick, glad there was something he *did* know. "She's carrying immigrants."

The boy pulled a face.

"What's the matter?" Dick asked.

"No lolly on that. You don't get no tips worth 'aving. And a right rough lot too, Irish labourers, Maltese, the lot."

"At the Shipping Federation Office the bloke said it was the only ship going."

"You got to make a start," said the boy. "If you 'aven't been to a Merchant Navy school or been to sea before that's the sort of ship you get."

His friend came back, carrying the glasses carefully.

"This bloke's joining the *Armada* next week," said the boy.

"I was on 'er a couple of years ago."

"Was she an immigrant ship?" Dick asked.

"No, we was on a trip to B.A."

"B.A.?"

"Buenos Aires."

It sounded romantic and far away. "Tell me," Dick said, "I been wondering, what do you 'ave to do?"

"What you joined as? Deck 'and?"

"Steward."

"Oh, you 'as to get up at five-thirty and lug the crates of drinks up to the bar. Then you do a bit of scrubbing, cleaning out the working alleyways. Then you 'as to lay up the tables for breakfast, then you 'as to serve two sittings, then you 'as your own grub. Then you 'as to lay up for lunch. If you're lucky there'll be an hour left before you start serving."

"What time's that?" asked Dick.

"First sitting's about twelve-thirty."

"You forgets scrubbing out the saloon and polishing the ports after breakfast," said the first boy. "And after lunch you 'as your own grub again, clear the tables and lay up for tea."

"You might get another hour on your own after that," said the boy who had done the trip to Buenos Aires. "Do a bit of sunbathing up on deck. Then you serves tea, lays up for dinner and serves that. After that you 'ave your own and the rest of the evening's yours."

The door of the bar opened and four men came in; three of them wore suits and satin ties and the other was in jeans and an open-necked shirt, his fingers covered with cheap rings.

"'Allo, Johnnie," he said to the boy Dick had spoken to first.

His eyes rested on Dick. "Mind if I sit next to you?"

Dick looked at him. "No."

The man sat down beside him, squashing on to the small seat. Dick could see he had powder on his face and a metal bracelet on his wrist. His open shirt revealed a silver cross on a chain like the one Reggie wore, and it nestled among the greying hairs on his chest. In contrast his hair was brilliantly blond. As he talked he played with the cross, twisting it between his fingers.

He turned to Johnnie and said, "Who's your friend?" He indicated Dick by sliding his eyes sideways in their sockets.

"I don't know 'is name," Johnnie said.

"My name's Dick," Dick said.

The men gave a chorus of giggles and shrieks and the one next to him said, "'Ow camp!"

Dick blushed.

"I love Dick," one screamed. And they all shrieked with laughter again.

"You'll 'ave to put Dick on the list, won't you?" said the man with rings.

"Listen to Mother."

"What list?" asked Dick.

"The queers list, dear. Mother keeps it in 'er cabin." They all laughed. "What ship you getting?"

"The *Armada*."

"Oh, my Gawd! Big Mary's on that ship, darling. You'll 'ave to do just what she says. She'll draw a knife if she's upset."

Dick thought. He can't mean a woman.

"Come on, Mother, drink up. We got to get a train."

The man with the rings finished his drink and they all swayed and minced out of the bar. Dick turned to Johnnie.

"Do they go to sea too, then?"

"Yeah, and dozens more."

Dick thought of the ugly, middle-aged powdered faces. He had never seen homosexuals like them before. He had never thought of his relationship with Reggie as being homosexual, he hadn't labelled it or questioned it. It wasn't like this. They would never be like these men. He thought he wouldn't really want to be at sea with people like that. Would he be able to keep out of their way, would they leave him and Reggie alone? He finished his drink too, said good-bye and went back to the station. As he walked along the platform he saw the men through the glass door of the refreshment room and heard their high-pitched laughter.

He walked to the end of the platform and when the train came in he saw them climb into a carriage and he got into a compartment next to the guard's van.

On the way home he thought about getting up so early and all the hard work and then about these awful queers. But he and Reggie would be able to stick it. It wasn't being alone like today. They would have each other. After Friday they wouldn't have to bother about anyone else.

TWELVE

Since Dot's visit to the café Dick and Reggie had often been followed by one or another of the gang. Les had tried to organize a full-scale shadowing operation like he had so frequently watched on films and on television. But it wasn't as easy as it looked and often the boys lost them, or found interests elsewhere and simply didn't bother to pursue them all evening.

Dick and Reggie were unaware of this, but nevertheless had become increasingly nervous and irritable, not only with other people but with themselves. It was so important that nothing should go wrong. They loved each other so much, they said, this was their one opportunity to stay together. There must be no mistakes. Every night they talked it over, worried and argued and in turn became confident and cocksure, then frightened and unsure and apprehensive. They had the tools ready, some stolen from the garage where Reggie worked, and some taken from Grand-dad's toolbox. They oiled and cleaned them, sharpened them, took them out and put them away again. They disagreed about the clothes they should wear and whether they should have masks. They became so angry they were on the point of fighting. Then the proximity turned the tension into desire and they said it was crazy to have a row, it was nerves. After Friday they would never fight again.

And on Friday, after a day that seemed endless, particularly to Dick who had nothing to do, and couldn't even sleep late and stay in bed as he usually did, they decided to go to Nick's.

"Les'll be wondering where we got to," Dick said. "We'd better show our noses." Quite apart from their feelings of guilt for bypassing the gang and their fear of giving themselves away, they no longer wanted any company except their own. They felt so close, so linked.

"Well, well, well," Les called out as they came into the café.

102

" 'Ere's a couple of strangers. Where you been, boys? We missed you."

Dick sensed the undertone uneasily, but Reggie smiled and said they'd been out on the bike getting a bit of fresh air, which was true.

"We was quite worried," Les said. "We thought you might 'ave got nabbed on the job."

"We ain't been on the job," Reggie said.

"Of course you 'aven't," Les agreed. "You wouldn't do anything without telling us, would you?"

" 'Course we wouldn't," Dick snapped. He wanted to leave.

"Come on," Reggie said, "let's 'ave a drink. I'm dry."

Les began to talk generally, drawing them into a conversation. He was unnaturally friendly, almost humbling himself, smiling and asking their opinions. Dick began to feel afraid. It seemed almost as if Les knew what they were going to do tonight. He had a sudden recollection of one of the gang at the cinema when he had been to see the layout of the place yesterday afternoon. But Les couldn't know. They hadn't told anyone.

When the clock struck half past eleven and Reggie stood up and said "Come on, mate, I'm dead beat, let's get some shut-eye," Dick wanted to run out of the café and jump on the bike and get right away.

"Good night," Les called. He smiled at them. "Sleep well."

"I'm sure 'e knows," Dick said nervously, as Reggie started the engine.

"Don't be mad. 'Ow could he?"

"There's something up. 'E's not like this other times."

"There's nothing up. You got the jitters, mate, that's all."

"Per'aps I 'ave." Dick was beginning to shiver although it was a warm night.

They drove away and out of the corner of his eye Dick saw another boy climb on his bike and drive off too, in the same direction. But there was nothing in it. Boys came and went all night. Other people had to go home too.

When the boy who was tailing them saw them go into Gran's house he thought for the moment that his work for the night was over. Then it occurred to him that on the previous occasion he had followed them home, Reggie had pulled the bike up the kerb and into the small front garden. Tonight he left it at the roadside. So the boy rode on past the house and waited at the end of the street, out of sight, in a builder's yard. Twenty minutes later he watched them come out again and ride away and he jerked his own bike out into the road and went after them. They turned into a side road, slowing down, and the boy tore past, shouting out good night to them. They answered and he thought that Dick's voice was shocked and not just surprised. Much further down the road he parked his own bike and began to walk back, but Dick and Reggie suddenly turned the corner and he just had time to duck into a front garden and hide behind the hedge as they passed. A dog in the house began to bark and Dick and Reggie started to run. Through the dark a man's voice shouted to the dog to be quiet and the boy slipped out of the gate and keeping close to the wall followed them. He felt he was doing something dangerous and important. He saw them stop outside the little Ritz cinema and then turn down the narrow alley to the side exit. The boy turned the way he had come and ran as fast as he could back to his bike.

"It's dead easy," Reggie said. His relief was tremendous. "You'd think they'd 'ave something stronger, wouldn't you?"

"They will next week, mate." Dick's confidence had returned.

The double door was secured by an expanding iron gate held by two padlocks. It had taken Reggie only a matter of minutes to saw through them with a file. He had the tools with him. He heaved the gate back and Dick held it while he forced open the door which was held by an iron bar latched across inside. But it wasn't secured and the bar soon slid back under the pressure from Reggie's shoulder. It made a loud clanging noise and they stood poised to run. But no one came and with renewed confidence they went into the cinema. Dick's torch picked out the large coloured photographs of film-stars on the walls. Their feet made no sound on the patterned carpet of the corridor. It was odd and eerie, being in a cinema quite by themselves. Dick pushed open the swing door of the auditorium and shone the torch down the aisle. The humped rows of seat-backs looked like tombstones. When he spoke to Reggie he whispered. His whisper seemed sibilant and on the edge of an echo. He let the door go and it swung backwards and forwards, making what seemed an immense amount of noise.

"Come on," Reggie said. "Which way?"

Dick walked slightly ahead to the foyer. The sweet kiosk was shuttered and the little glass panel of the box office was down.

104

"There, mate," Dick said. He pointed to a door marked MANAGER. He went over to it and turned the handle and to his amazement the door opened and they went in.

"Not even bloody locked," said Reggie. Dick shone the torch round the room. Under the window, squat, prominent, was a safe, fixed to the floor, the carpet round it cut away in a neat square.

"It's a present," said Dick. " 'E's given it us." He felt like laughing. It was so easy.

Reggie knelt down beside the safe and tipped his tools out of the little bicycle-repair bag. He began to lever at the lock.

"You can do it, can't you?" said Dick. He began to pull open the drawers of the desk. "Not much worth 'aving 'ere."

Reggie prized and pushed and attacked. Dick stood beside him, suddenly impatient, a little afraid.

"Come on, Reggie, we ain't got all night."

"I know, I know." Reggie was sweating. He tried one tool after another, and they kept slipping and sticking into his left hand. "F.... thing. These tools are no good. You need gelly, not a bloody screwdriver. You didn't say it was a safe."

"I didn't know, did I? I couldn't come *in* here, could I?" His voice rose.

"Well, it's no good." Reggie stood up and flung his tools on to the floor. "We might as well go 'ome. We won't get a brass farthing out of this place."

"Shall we try the box office, then?" Dick pleaded. He felt tears pricking at his eyes. Everything would go wrong now. There would be no money, no Merchant Navy, they wouldn't be able to stay together. Reggie would never agree to doing anything like this again, he was so stubborn, so bloody set on being honest. "Don't let's pack it in yet, Reggie." He couldn't keep the desperation out of his voice. He shounded shrill and panicking.

"I've 'ad enough." Reggie bent down and picked up his things and walked out of the little office without looking at Dick.

Dick hurried after him, almost running. "Let's take some fags, Reggie. There's the counter. Let's take something. Shall we try something else?"

"No we won't. I never did like doing it and this 'as f—ing finished me for good and all." As he spoke he knew he was hurting Dick, but he was so disappointed he couldn't conceal his feelings. He didn't know what to do. You didn't get any-

105

where if you didn't go straight. If he hadn't got anything else out of it he had learnt that lesson. He hurried on ahead of Dick. He couldn't look at him. He couldn't have met Dick's eyes.

Dick couldn't speak. If he spoke he knew he would cry. He wanted to say to Reggie, do you still love me, will you still join the Merchant Navy with me, you won't leave me now, because of this, will you? But he was so afraid Reggie would say, it's all finished, mate, it was a bloody mistake, mate. Better to wait until they were in bed and Reggie wasn't angry any more. A tear ran down Dick's face and into the corner of his mouth. He swallowed hard. Reggie would think he was mad.

In silence they let themselves out of the side door and it closed behind them, on its spring hinges. Reggie held the iron gate back for Dick, and as Dick passed him their shoulders brushed. Then Dick walked ahead of him along the alley and into the street where they had left the bike. Neither of them spoke again. They turned the corner.

Dick stopped. "The bike's gone," he said. He was suddenly on the verge of hysteria. "The bike's been taken, Reggie."

" 'Oo could 'ave taken it, darlin'?" It was Les's voice behind them.

They spun round. He stood there, legs apart, arms outstretched. Dick's mouth went dry.

" 'Ave you been mucking about with the bike?" Reggie demanded.

"I didn't come 'ere to muck the bike up," Les said. He took a step forward. "You little sods," he said, "you don't do no jobs without me." And he brought up his left fist and crashed it into Reggie's jaw.

"Leave 'im alone," Dick screamed. "We didn't take no money. Leave 'im alone."

"Come on, cats," Les shouted. "Let's show 'em what 'appens when they go on their own."

Dick turned sharply. Boys were coming out of every shadow, out of the public lavatory at the side of the road, vaulting the fence of the school recreation ground, behind Les, behind Reggie. Reggie had staggered but now he flung himself at Les, punching him hard in the chest and throat. Dick turned and began to run. I must get help, he sobbed to himself, I must get the law. His head throbbed. His throat constricted. Boys closed in on him, closed in on Reggie, boys in black leather with razor blades and bicycle chains. They thudded after Dick and caught him, they

106

pulled Reggie away from Les and threw him on to the ground. Hands pulled at him and hurt him and he fell and they seemed to cover him so that he could see nothing but legs and feet and arms. He felt the boots kicking into him, into his thighs and testicles and stomach. He screamed out with pain but they went on and on and on. Then the boys moved aside and only Les was there, and for a split second before the blow he saw Les's boot above his face.

"Law!"

The knot of boys spread out and scattered. They ran in all directions, dodging the groups of people in pyjamas and dressing-gowns who were standing at both ends of the street. A policeman on a little grey motor-cycle tore past them to where Dick and Reggie lay in the middle of the road.

Slowly, painfully, Dick began to try to stand. Every part of him felt swollen and agonized. He could barely see. His lips were stiff. He pulled himself, half standing, half falling, to where Reggie was lying on his side, his legs bent, his jeans and jacket lacerated. Dick dropped on to his knees beside him. The effort was almost overbearing and he collapsed on to Reggie's chest.

The policeman stood over him, towering away like a tree. The bell of a police car penetrated Dick's brain, cutting into the murmur of voices he hadn't been aware of until now. He blinked and Reggie's face came into focus under the yellow lights of the street lamps. Black lines seemed to have been drawn thinly from the corners of his eyes and mouth and nose. Blood, he said to himself. He couldn't keep his eyes open for long.

Hands were under his armpits, helping him to his feet.

"We'll get this lot," said a voice. "They deserve all they get and more." The helping hands weren't gentle. "Go on, see if the other one's coming round."

Dick saw a second policeman shake Reggie. Shake him again, and then abruptly stop. "Christ!" he said. "Christ, come and have a look over here. He's had it. This one's had it. He's dead."

The white square of an ambulance came into Dick's vision, and the doors opened and someone was helping him into a scarlet dotted void. Dead, dead, dead. Someone was taking off his jacket, rolling up what was left of his sleeve, sticking a needle into his arm. Lying on a stretcher wrapped in a blanket, he was aware of activity outside which seemed to go on for hours. Then he was aware of another stretcher being brought in and placed opposite him. He tried to raise himself up enough to see.

His arms were like cotton wool. Tears were pouring down his face. There was only a scarlet blanket, about six foot long, rounded neatly at the top and divided into two peaks at the bottom by the pointed toes of a pair of boots.

THIRTEEN

Dick opened his eyes. There were screens round his bed covered in blue material. Quite close to him sat a man in a grey suit. Dick closed his eyes again. He heard the man stand up, scraping his chair on the polished floor, and looking saw him disappear through a gap in the screens. In a moment he returned with a nurse whose face was pink and round, and Dick's eyes hurt so much he couldn't open them wide enough to see her features.

"Open your mouth," said the nurse. "I want to take your temperature before Doctor comes."

The thermometer hurt his tongue. He hurt all over, even the slightest movement made a pain, blinking his eyes or lifting his tongue. He lay there, hurting, remembering slowly with a terrifying fear and desolation. The moments seemed to have no duration, he was unaware of time, if it was minutes or hours before the doctor came and touched him, lifting his wrist, shining a torch into his eyes, placing the icy trumpet of a stethoscope on to his burning chest.

"I'm sorry," the doctor said to the man in the grey suit. "He's not up to it. You'll have to hang on a bit longer." And Dick sank back into a dreamless sleep.

When he had next woken the man was still there. And this time Dick talked to him. He was a C.I.D. officer and he wanted a statement. He wanted to know exactly what had happened on Friday night; he wanted to know why the gang had attacked them. For a moment Dick considered lying. Then he thought, Reggie's dead. And there was no point. Now there was only himself to go to prison and he didn't care if he went to prison or not. He didn't care if he went to prison or went home or died too. So he told the truth about how he and Reggie had broken into the cinema and that somehow Les had found out.

"You going to 'ave me for that?" he said. "Breaking in and that?"

109

"Don't worry, Dick," said the officer. He had called him Dick all the time. "It's the others we wanted, and we've got them. We'll leave you to get better." And he told him that next Friday he would have to come to court when Les and the four boys arrested with him would be charged.

"With murder?" Dick asked. But the man wouldn't tell him.

"Do what the doctor says, and be well enough to come without a wheelchair." Then he added. "Oh, and by the way, we've got your bike safe and sound. One of the boys will drop it round to your home, if you like."

The bike. He lay and thought about it. They thought it was his. Well, they would find out sooner or later that it wasn't, but he would hang on to it until they did. No point in telling them it was Reggie's. The thought of owning a bike, even temporarily, even while he felt so bruised he couldn't have worked an invalid carriage, was thrilling. For a second he forgot Reggie. Then he thought it would remind him of Reggie just to see it. The sound, the smell, the feel of it would recall Reggie. But it would be different, he told himself, driving it, being in control, not just a passenger on the pillion, holding on to Reggie, seeing the back of his neck and the short fair hair under the crash helmet. Oh Jesus, he wanted Reggie. Hot tears fell on to his pillow, making his eyes and throat ache. He wouldn't have believed he could cry so much, just like a kid. Reggie, he thought, oh, Reggie, come back, don't be dead. Dead. He turned on to his side and put his face into the pillow.

"Come on now, Mr. Smith, you won't get better this way." The nurse was standing there, and he turned his head back to look at her. He didn't answer her, and made an effort to control his crying.

"How about a nice cup of tea? Or hot milk? Would you like something now?" He shook his head. "Well, all right, but no more of that noise or we'll have the patients complaining, and then we'll all be in trouble. Even Matron will get to hear of it." She smiled cheerfully. "Understand now, not another squeak. Mr. Potter in the next bed is trying to get some sleep."

Now, days later, his stitches were out and he was on his way home. He had been taken to court by ambulance, and made his statement, and heard Les being charged with murder, because it was Les's final kick, the pathologist said, which had killed

110

Reggie. Dick had seen Les administer the kick. He was an important witness. It seemed that the whole episode had been a dream. It began with meeting Reggie and ended when he woke in hospital, and of course he hadn't met Reggie at all. Reggie had never been real, never been in Nick's café or at the seaside or in bed, he was only in this dream.

Home was with his parents again, at least until after the trial; the police and the hospital almoner had arranged that. He didn't know what he would do when the trial was over he certainly wouldn't – couldn't – stay at home, he might still join the Merchant Navy as they had planned to do. He remembered how excited he and Reggie had been when he had come back from Southampton and told Reggie about the ship. They had wondered what clothes they should take with them, how they set about joining a union, how long they would have to be on board before the ship sailed, how they would break the news to Gran.

"Wait till we passes our medicals before we worry 'er," Reggie had said.

Dick still wondered how the gang had found out, whether he would ever know. He felt that he was the one who was ultimately responsible for Reggie's death, because if Reggie hadn't fallen in love with him, he would never have wanted to get right away, and would never have needed the money to give to Dot. He sat in the bus, his head in his hands. He thought he would never, never get over loving Reggie.

Dick sat on a bench in the enormous first-floor lobby of the Old Bailey, waiting to be called as a witness. Opposite him was the double door of the court, and every now and then, when someone went in or out, he could see a policeman sitting just inside. He had always been a bit wary of the law. Now he seemed to be on their side. On his left was a statue of Elizabeth Fry. He didn't know who Elizabeth Fry was, any more than he knew what the coloured murals on the upper parts of the walls depicted. But Elizabeth Fry's name was on the base of the statue. He had walked over to see. He had thought it was Florence Nightingale, the only woman in history that he remembered. All the way up the stairs, with its gleaming brass handrail, were busts of men standing on tall plinths, rather like the standing ashtrays in Les's sister's flat. Downstairs in the entrance hall, in groups on the white marble floor inset with huge black circles and triangles, were men in lounge suits and gowns. Upstairs were several people like himself, waiting anxiously on the wooden benches. He still felt weak and shaken, and the scar on his face hurt as much as it did on the day the stitches were taken out. Every morning when he woke up he ached to have Reggie with him. The realization that he was dead, that he would never see him again, kept recurring and recurring, so that when he was doing ordinary things like combing his hair or drinking tea, the memory returned and he felt sick and his eyes stung and a weight seemed to drop from his chest down to his stomach. Already he could not recall Reggie's voice and he knew that soon he would only be able to visualize him inaccurately. There was no way of keeping Reggie.

Dot sat in the public gallery of number one court. She had queued for several hours to get in, standing with a horde of excited women. She had tramped up endless flights of stairs with them, past the policeman at the door. And she had got a front seat. She sat looking down on to the half-empty court. She wore a cotton skirt over a stiff petticoat and a tight cotton sweater. Boys had whistled at her as she had waited for the bus but she had never felt less provocative in her life. She knew that it had been her fault. When Carol had showed her the *Daily Mirror* at work on Saturday morning she thought she was going to die. Her mouth had gone dry, she had felt so weak she had had to lean against the counter and her hand had knocked over a tray of yoghourt cartons. Reggie! Reggie killed! "I did it," she said to Carol. "I did it, didn't I?" She had gone to the doctor for sleeping pills and tranquillizers and had gone home to her mother. But now she had her widow's pension, which came in useful, and had gained prestige and no one knew Reggie had left her and it didn't seem so bad. The shock was over. Reporters had sought her out and she had been quoted in various papers as saying "he wouldn't hurt a fly" and "his favourite dinner was a pork chop". She was due to have a session with a feature writer of a Sunday paper for an article called "My Teen-age Husband was Murdered".

From where she sat in the gallery she could see the jury filing into the box as the usher called their names. She looked at the tops of their heads: two bald, four thinning, one thick and grey, one thick and black, three hats, one grey bun. In turn they took the oath. One man was Jewish and spread his pocket handkerchief on his head. In the well of the court a number of men

112

wearing wigs and gowns were arranging their papers. The women round her were talking excitedly with a familiarity of the procedure and a pleasure that Dot found frightening. They were like flies round a dead dog. They went to murder trials like she went to the cinema. They were enjoying Reggie's horrible death, it thrilled them. It made her sick.

The usher, gowned but not wigged, shouted for silence. The hubbub of voices subsided. The door at the front of the court which led on to the raised platform where the Judge was to sit, opened, and the Judge and his procession entered. Everyone in the court stood up. The Judge wore red robes and glasses. His face was red too. One of his escorts carried a sword, another a cocked hat under his arm. The Judge himself carried a little nosegay of flowers. He bowed, and the wigged barristers bowed back. He sat down on the large throne-like chair. It was set slightly in front of the other chairs which were covered, like this one, in green leather and had wooden arms that matched the panelling of the courtroom. The procession, excepting the Judge, passed out of the door at the other end of the platform, and the Clerk of the Court, whose desk was below the Judge but higher than everyone else, stood and began to call the names of the defendants. With a sense of guilt Dot saw Les and the other boys escorted into the dock by two warders wearing long looped key chains. There was a rustle among the observers and some coughing. The case had begun.

Dick wondered how long it would be before he was called. The other people, a mother and father and a fat pregnant daughter with a long frizz of fair hair, who had been sitting with him, had gone. He had gone to the local café for lunch, but he hadn't been able to eat and had come back and waited for the court to assemble again. It had been in session for an hour and still no one had come for him. He thought how different it was to the Magistrates' Court. There he had waited in a grubby corridor with a collection of tarts and tramps and drunks. A child had been sick on the floor, and smacked by its mother. No one came to clean up the mess and it had been spread. Here it was grand and formal and the people who hurried through the lobby were mostly grand too, and aloof, and even the witnesses were hushed. He wished he could go inside and listen. He was nervous at the thought of giving evidence, apprehensive of seeing Les at the trial. He hated Les, he was afraid of him. It would be strange and terrifying to see him subservient and afraid too. The fight seemed so long ago, impossible that people as insignificant as himself and Reggie should have been the cause of all that was happening today, and that the Judge and the solicitors and the barristers and the reporters and the public should be doing what they were doing, waiting for the evening papers to come out, because he and Reggie had broken into the little Ritz cinema.

FOURTEEN

"CALL Richard Arthur Smith."

This was the moment Dick had been dreading. He went through the swinging doors, past the back benches where previous witnesses now sat, past the jury to the witness-box. A little microphone was suspended in front of him. He took the oath as he had done in the Magistrates' Court. Down below the wigged barristers were seated at their tables. In the dock, with its locked door and high walls, was Les, just as he had imagined. The others were sitting there too, and they had pieces of blank paper on the ledge in front of them. Dave had screwed his into a little ball.

One of the wigged men stood up and faced Dick.

"Richard Arthur Smith?"

"Yes," Dick said quietly. He hoped he could be heard. He couldn't have spoken any louder. It was an effort to say anything at all.

"Mr. Smith, I want to take your mind back to the evening of Friday, June the sixth, at about half past nine, when, I understand, you and Reginald Rogers went into a café called Nick's Bar, where you met, among others, the five youths you see standing in the dock."

"That's correct," said Dick. He spoke in a manner that wasn't natural to him. "Correct" was not a word he would normally use.

"I should like you to tell me what happened following that meeting."

"Well," Dick began, "we 'ad a few drinks . . ."

"Not intoxicating drinks?"

"Oh no. Coke and that. You can't buy liquor at Nick's. Well, after we'd 'ad these drinks we said good night and went off on the bike to my Gran's 'ouse."

"Had you, at this point, any inkling of what was to follow?"

115

"Oh no," Dick said. "I was a bit nervy, but I didn't think nothing was up. We went to the 'ouse to get our things."

"Things?"

"A little bag of tools for forcing locks and things."

"Would you tell the court why you had the tools?"

"Reggie and me was going to do the Ritz . . ."

The Judge leaned forward and gave a little cough. "I'm afraid I don't quite understand. *Do the Ritz?*"

"Break into it. Do it," Dick said impatiently. "We was going to do the Ritz."

"Surely that was rather ambitious," the Judge said, smiling around.

"If I may elucidate," said the Counsel.

"Do, do, please, Mr. Carstairs."

"The Ritz is a small cinema in Flora Road. It is marked on map A."

The Judge ruffled his papers, found the map and studied it for almost a minute.

"May we continue, your honour?"

"Yes, please do." The Judge set the paper on top of the pile of others and sat back, listening.

"Why did you intend to break into this cinema?" the Counsel asked, turning back to Dick who had been puzzled by this interchange.

"We needed money, you see," Dick said. "My Gran was in 'ospital and Reggie wanted to give his wife some. 'E'd left 'er and wanted to make sure she was all right if you get me."

"I get you." There was a stir of laughter. "Although you intended to steal it wasn't for yourselves you wanted the money."

"That's right, sir." He remembered suddenly that he had been told by the police to say "Sir".

The Prosecuting Counsel seemed pleased and he looked at his papers and smiled at Dick before he went on:

"You collected the tools from the house?"

"Yes. Then we got on the bike and went down to the Ritz."

"To Flora Road, that is?" said the Judge referring to his map again.

"Yes, sir."

"Were you aware that you were being followed?" asked the Counsel.

"No."

"Not at any time?"

116

"No. Bill passed us." For a second his eyes met Bill's across the court. "But 'e didn't stop. Just called good night. I didn't think 'e was following us."

"And then?"

"We parked the bike a couple of streets away and walked to the Ritz. Then we broke in, but we couldn't get any money so we came out again and walked back to the bike."

"And was your bike where you had left it?"

"No. It 'ad gone. And I said, 'The bike's gone,' and Les came up be'ind us and said, 'I wonder 'oo took it?' or something like that. And Reggie said, ' 'Ave you been messing about with the bike?' and 'e said, 'I'm going to mess about with you too.' That's not the exact words, sir. 'E said something like that." As he spoke it came back so clearly that Dick found himself trembling. "Then the others all come out from where they was 'iding and got 'old of me and Reggie and beat us up."

"Now," the Prosecuting Counsel said slowly and kindly, "I want you to remember exactly what happened during the fight. After the other boys appeared, what happened then?" He reminded Dick of his old headmaster. When you were really in trouble he spoke quietly, like this, asking you to tell the truth. He never shouted or scared you.

"They all come round Reggie, and I started to run off, but they saw me and some of 'em left Reggie and come after me."

"What did they do to Reggie?"

"I couldn't see much. I kept getting punched and 'it, and someone 'ad a blade and cut me face and 'ands." He touched the scar on his cheek. "I fell down."

"Did you see what was happening to him at all?"

"When I fell I saw 'e was on the ground too, and 'e was crying, sort of screaming."

"He was definitely crying out at this point?"

"Yes, sir. 'E cried, 'Stop it, you're 'urting me.' " Dick's voice shook.

"Then what happened?"

"Les left me and went over to where Reggie was and the boys got out of 'is way. They always do when Les is coming. I saw 'im kick Reggie. Then I sort of passed out, only for a few seconds. Then the police come and they all tried to run off, and the ambulance came."

"Did you see Reggie before you were taken to the ambulance?"

It seemed odd to hear the Counsel call him Reggie, as if he knew him too.

"Yes. I went over to 'im."

"Was he dead?"

"I didn't think 'e was dead," Dick almost whispered. "I never thought 'e was dead."

"But you knew he was alive before Green went across and kicked him?"

"Yes."

"Thank you." He sat down.

Dick was sweating, but he felt very cold. It was terrible remembering when he wanted to put it out of his mind more than anything in the world.

The Defending Counsel for Les stood up. He was a tall, thin man with a clipped moustache.

"You said just now, Mr. Smith, that after you had seen Leslie Green kick Rogers, you 'passed out'. If you passed out how do you know that somebody else didn't administer a further and possibly fatal blow?"

"I only passed out for a moment, sir."

"How do you know it was only a moment? If you were unconscious you couldn't be aware of the time."

"I sort of come over dizzy," Dick said. "I put my 'ead down on the road. I couldn't see. I wasn't right out, not like being asleep, I mean."

"Yet you say the moment before that you *saw* the accused kick Rogers?"

"Yes, sir."

"If you were in a condition that caused you to become unconscious, even momentarily – and there is no evidence that it *was* momentarily – how can you be certain that it was Green kicking Rogers and not one of the other boys? If you were dizzy, how could you tell clearly who it was?"

"I know it was 'im."

"What was he wearing?"

"Motor-cycle kit."

"What were the other boys wearing? What were you yourself wearing?"

"Motor-cycle kit."

"Exactly. All of you were wearing the same kind of clothes."

"Les 'ad a tiger's 'ead painted on 'is."

"Did you see the tiger's head on the back of the person kicking Rogers?"

"I might 'ave done," Dick said. "I know it was Les."

"In a few minutes, Mr. Smith, you will be convinced that you saw the tiger's head. You will say that you must have seen the tiger's head to have identified Green."

"I know it was 'im." Dick was angry and frustrated. His voice was raised. "I recognized 'im."

"You recognized him?" said Les's Defending Counsel. His grey eyebrows shot up under his grey wig. "You *recognized* him when you were dizzy and on the point of unconsciousness? Why, it could have been any one of the boys standing there, or, indeed, a boy *not* standing there in the dock today. I suggest you were in no state to distinguish one similarly clad boy from another."

Dot thought, How much longer are they going on? Dick had been questioned for two hours now, and the questions seemed repetitive and pointless and half of them she couldn't really comprehend. I don't get it, she said to herself several times. He's just said that, and the other bloke said it too. Why do they ask him again? She knew from earlier cross-examining that each of the five boys on trial had a Counsel to defend him. Only one had cross-examined Dick. Her previous knowledge of court procedure came from American films and she was astonished how long this was taking. She was plain bored by it all. If she hadn't felt so guilty she would have packed it in at lunchtime. But she had to stay and hear it out.

"We will adjourn until tomorrow morning," said the Judge. And Dot stood with the rest of the women in the gallery and then began to edge her way out to the stairs.

In the lobby Dick met the C.I.D. officer who had been in charge of the case, and who had taken his statement in hospital. For Dick it was like meeting an old friend. He felt exhausted and nervous and in an alien world. The officer gave Dick a thumbs-up sign.

"You're doing fine," he said.

" 'Ow long will it go on for?" Dick asked. "I can't take much more."

"It'll be over by tomorrow. You'll see. We'll have it all wrapped up by this time tomorrow."

" 'E makes out I'm lying all the time," Dick said. "And 'e

119

said I wasn't honest and not to believe me." He was very indignant. "Well, 'e made it out, like, without saying it."

"Don't worry," said the officer. "If they haven't got a case they always try to blacken the witnesses or the police. He knows he hasn't a chance. He's just wasting everyone's time."

"It all goes in the papers," Dick said, still thinking of his own character. "My Gran'll think it's true."

"Wait till tomorrow," the officer said. "You'll be all right then."

Chairs had been brought in for the family from another ward. Nothing was too much trouble for Gran, poor old girl, the nurses said. Awful having her grandson mixed up in this terrible murder. But Dick had acquired the reputation of a film-star and Gran had had photographs of him as a baby brought from her home and everyone said what a lovely little chap he'd been. The family had come to the hospital today because the verdict was expected and Gran would get it over her earphones. It was almost as if Dick was in the dock, and it was *his* verdict they were waiting for. Gran was often up now, for almost a day at a time. Soon she would be coming out and going to a convalescent home by the sea for three weeks.

"Decided what you're going to do after that, Mum?" Dick's mother asked nervously. She felt sure that someone, she didn't know who, the sister or the almoner or a welfare worker, was going to approach her and tell her it was her duty to put a bed in her front room and give it over to Gran.

"Well, I 'ave." Gran settled back on her nest of four pillows. She smiled a little. "The almoner said as I ought to go to you. She said I didn't ought to be on me own no more."

"What about Dick?" Dick's mother said. "Perhaps 'e'll come back to you. 'E's a good boy," she said, forgetting, in her anxiety.

"Dick wouldn't come back to me now," Gran said. " 'E 'asn't come to see me, not since all this 'appened."

" 'E's ashamed of 'isself," Dick's mother said. "When it's all over 'e'll settle down again."

"No," Gran said. " 'E goes out nights and I must 'ave some one with me nights." She paused, enjoying Dick's mother's expression. Do her good to have a fright, mean old bitch, she said to herself. "The almoner said I must 'ave someone with me nights. But I told 'er I wouldn't go to you if it was the last

120

place on earth. I only go where I'm welcome, I said. So she come up with the idea that I let me top room, very cheap, to some nice lady 'oo'll fill me 'ot-water bottle and keep an eye on me. Do a bit of shopping and that." Dick's mother's mouth fell open with relief. "She even thinks she can find a nice lady for me. One 'oo's been in 'ere, so we'll 'ave something to chat about."

Dick's mother's voice was high and affable. "What a lovely idea, Mum. 'Ow clever to think it up then."

"Put on your 'eadphones," said Dick's father. "It's time for the news. And let's 'ave one of them chocs while we're waiting."

"What puzzles me," said the Counsel for the boy with the shaved head – from the gallery Dot could see the beginnings of stubble all over his crown – "is that earlier on you assured me that you didn't know which of the boys were attacking you and which were attacking Rogers. Yet now you say Baxter" (Baxter was the name of the boy with the shaved head. Dick hadn't known that until today) "was with the gang attacking Rogers. While we are aware he was with the gang on that night we have no proof that he administered any blow at all to Rogers. Thank you. I have no more questions."

They had all finished with Dick. He was told he could leave the box. It was three o'clock. Except for the lunch break he had been there all day. He went to the seats at the side of the court. He had only had a cup of tea since morning and he felt ill and exhausted. He watched the last witness go into the box, the man who had called the police to the scene of the fight. He began his evidence. He was asleep, he said, in his house at the corner of the road, but he had been awakened by terrible shouting. He had gone to the window and seen what appeared to be two groups of fighting boys. He had wakened his wife. She said he must call the police, so he put on his dressing-gown and went downstairs.

Dick thought, I've had enough. I don't want to know any more. He waited until the man left the box and then he walked out of the courtroom and down the stairs and out into the street. He took a big breath of air. He wished it was all over. He wished it was years ago and life between had been full and this was a memory and didn't matter, in the way Grand-dad's dying didn't matter any longer. He crossed the street and went into the café on the corner.

121

Dot saw Dick leave the court and after a moment she stood up too and left the gallery and the policeman opened the door for her. She ran along the passage, past the standing board saying COURT FULL – for this was a popular case – and down the flights of steps. In the street she looked for Dick but couldn't see him. She didn't know what she was going to say, whether or not she was going to confess to Reggie's mate that she had told Les, whether she was just going to talk about the trial, or if, when actually confronted with Dick, she would have the nerve to speak at all. He's probably gone for a cup of tea, she thought. He must be dry after all that talking. She went over to the café and stood inside the door. Dick was in the queue at the counter and she went over to him.

"I'm Dot," she said, "Reggie's wife. Could you get me a cup of tea too?" Even as she spoke she thought, it could be quite romantic, meeting like this. Dick jumped and looked round, stared at her and nodded. She was sorry she had taken him by surprise but it was the way they always did things in films and in books too. She called her comics "books". She sat down at a table and waited for him to come over. When he did, carrying a tray, she pushed his chair out for him and lifted the cups off the tray and on to the table. He put the tray on end against the table legs and sat down.

"You 'ad a long time in there," she said.

He nodded. He hated her. She was so ugly, that smeary mouth and dry hair. How could Reggie have married her, even long ago, even before they had met each other?

"What did you come for?" he asked her. "I wouldn't 'ave come if I didn't 'ave to."

She thought, I'll tell him now. I'll tell him why I came. She felt burdened with guilt.

"You watched it all, then?" Dick said.

"Yeah. 'E was trying to make out you was lying, the last one."

"They all were. But I know what I saw."

" 'Course you did." The moment had passed. She couldn't tell him now. "You was with Reggie a lot, wasn't you?"

"Yeah, that's right." Dick suddenly thought about the bike. She probably knew he had the bike and wanted it back. They drank their tea in silence. A woman with a large face framed by sausage curls under an almost invisible hair-net sat at their table and unloaded a portion of jam tart and a currant bun and a cup of tea from her tray.

"You going back in there?" Dot asked.

"No. I can read it in the papers."

"Don't you want to know what they get? They was summing up by the time I got out."

He shook his head. "I don't want to go back in there again."

Dot felt her last chance of talking to Dick was going, that if she failed now in establishing some sort of future relationship she would never seen him again. He was watching her suspiciously.

"Will you be 'ere for long, then?" she said.

"I might."

"I'll come back and tell you what's 'appened, shall I?"

"All right." He watched her go to the door. He was curiously unmoved by her, not jealous now, not repelled as he had been at first. He reached out his hand for the sugar castor and shook it over his cup.

Dot said to the policeman, "Can I come in again?"

"Your seat's still there."

She smiled thankfully, and walked down the steep steps to the front of the gallery, and the women in the row moved up to make room for her at the end. The Judge had gone. The jury-box was empty. Then the door opened and the jury returned and the woman next to Dot said, "Only half an hour. Fancy!" The Judge came back too, and took his seat, and asked the jury if they had agreed on a verdict.

"We have, sir."

"Do you find the prisoners at the bar guilty or not guilty?"

"Guilty, sir."

There was whispering and talking. "No other verdict, was there, I said all along," said the woman sitting next to Dot.

The Judge leaned forward slightly, and took off his glasses, laying them on the pile of papers on the desk in front of him.

"Before I pass sentence," he said slowly, "I find it necessary to allow myself a few comments on the case in question." He spoke as if this was the most important moment of the trial. He had obviously been waiting for it. He went on, "Not because it is in any way unique, but because it is not. Because it is one which may be said to be appallingly regular, one which has no outstanding aspects involving curious circumstances or even elaborate points of law." What does he mean? thought Dot, trying to listen so that she could report to Dick afterwards. "Unhappily, as I have said, it falls into an alarmingly familiar pattern, where young men, sometimes committing a breach of the law – " (Breach. She knew the word "breach". It meant upside down. People had breach babies. Mum said she'd been a breach.) " – sometimes not, are anxious to commit violence of an extreme order upon one another, culminating in the death of one of them."

Dot looked at the five boys in the dock. The two warders seemed to be unaware of what was taking place. They sat with their eyes down. Only when Dave moved his legs did they look up.

"Other voices in other places have been raised at this particular malaise of our time," said the Judge. He looked towards the reporters scribbling in their notebooks. No doubt, even as he spoke the words, he saw the evening newspaper headlines ("*Malaise of our Time*," *says Judge*). "It is not for me to examine the social reasons nor to probe the roots of this evil growth" (*This Evil Growth*), "but to pass judgement upon those of you who have manifested it." He spoke directly to the boys in the box. "Perhaps in these last few weeks you have had a chance to turn your thoughts inwardly and to think about the tragic waste, the stupidity, the pointlessness, of what you have done. Perhaps not. If that be so, I hope that what I am saying now may make you do so. That healthy young men in no way deprived of the basic needs of life should so misdirect themselves through aimlessness, wantonness and malevolence as to bring about the death of another is a wrong which, surely, must be apparent to you at moments when you have the courage to face your consciences." Their faces were quite blank, not from indifference but because they did not understand the Judge's elaborate phraseology.

"Leslie Gary Green, the jury has found you guilty of murder and I hereby sentence you to fourteen years' imprisonment."

Dot looked down at Les. He understood that. He started, turned to look at the other boys and grinned. The reporters watched and wrote busily. The Judge proceeded to sentence the rest of them, nine years for the boy with the shaved head, six for Dave and the two youngest were placed on probation.

"I have dealt with you all as leniently as the law allows," the Judge concluded, "because nothing I or anyone else can do will bring back the young man you have done to death. It can only be hoped that in the future that lies before you, you will begin to

124

realize the magnitude of the misery that you have introduced into the lives of so many people."

Dick finished drinking and put the plastic cup back on to the saucer, into a little pool of slopped tea. He wondered if the case was over, but realized at once that it couldn't be because no one was coming out of the courts. He half wished he had gone back, but a glance at the ponderous entrance seemed to bring about such constriction of his limbs that he knew he could not have mounted the steps again.

He left the café and crossed to the centre of the road where the bike was parked by the public lavatories which formed an island opposite the courts. He drew on his leather gloves, pulled the strap of his crash helmet tightly under his chin, swung his leg over the saddle and kick-started the machine. The very act of gripping the handle-bars and feeling the engine beating beneath him promised a liberation from all that had happened. It was comforting to realize his ability to get away, rapidly, alone. Away from Dot, and the threat that she might take the bike away, away from Les. But even moving out from the shadow of the Old Bailey, through the grey streets, did not remove the tightness from his chest, a physical feeling he had carried with him ever since he had woken in the hospital bed. As he had lain there he had wondered if it was a bruise, but as he had got better he had realized it was an ache of a different sort, an ache compounded of loneliness and guilt. At no point in the last weeks had anybody questioned his association with Reggie, and there had been times when he had wanted to blurt out, cry out, we loved each other. But he couldn't. There was no one, no one, no one he could tell.

He rode slowly down to Ludgate Circus, along New Bridge Street and across Blackfriars Bridge. To the right the river glittered in a grey curve towards the towers of Westminster, the new buildings of the South Bank. To the left a cluster of gulls wheeled over Blackfriars Railway Bridge. He thought again of the plans they had made to go to sea. It seemed now the only thing he could do, the only way to get away, perhaps even find Reggie. As he rode at an unaccustomedly slow pace through the streets of South London he thought how quick and simple it all seemed. He would sell the bike and send the money to Gran and take a train to Southampton and get a ship, any ship, anywhere.

He pulled up for some traffic lights. Another motor-cycle drew up alongside him. It was new and powerful. The young man astride it wore an immaculate leather jacket, a heavy leather belt, leather jeans and ankle-length boots. His crash helmet was silver with a black skull painted on the side. He revved his engine while waiting for the lights to change. Neither he nor Dick looked at each other but kept their eyes on the stop light, each accepting the unspoken challenge. The light changed to amber, and both machines roared away in unison, their exhausts clattering and reverberating, the smell of burnt fuel lingering in the air.

The Liberty Man

by Gillian Freeman

A sailor ashore – with money in his pocket – and a pretty girl who is lonely.

But the sailor is an East End boy and the girl is the daughter of a middle-class home. They become lovers, drawn together by desire and their youth. Can the affair outlast the physical attraction and all the differences between them?

". . . describes, convincingly and touchingly, the brief sensual affair that springs up . . . their frank attraction for each other is given a warm and compelling context . . . a novel that has the ring of truth." – *The Times Literary Supplement*

FOUR SQUARE EDITION 3s. 6d.